Dedication

This book is dedicated to the United States Coast Guard Rescue Swimmers. Thank you for doing what you do every day. *Semper Paratus*

And to my wife: Without you, I wouldn't be where I am today. *Je t'aime.*

Never Let Go

By

Graysen Morgen

2016

Never let Go © 2016 **Graysen Morgen**
Triplicity Publishing, LLC

ISBN-13: 978-0997740509
ISBN-10: 0997740507

Printed in the United States of America
First Edition – 2016
Cover Design: Triplicity Publishing, LLC
Interior Design: Triplicity Publishing, LLC
Editor: Megan Brady - Triplicity Publishing, LLC

Acknowledgements

Special thanks to my editor, Megan Brady. I'm glad we were finally able to work together.
Gratias!

Chapter 1

It was a hot and humid, sticky summer night in Merritt Island, Florida, and it was barely June. Finley Morris ran a hand through her tousled, curly, dark hair. She kept it fairly short, because as a Helicopter Rescue Swimmer in the United States Coast Guard, having long hair would be a complete nuisance. Her breasts were smaller than average and only visible under her dress uniform, but she was lean and physically fit. Finley didn't miss a day without running three to four miles, plus hitting the weights in the gym—a rigorous workout routine that kept her in shape to be able to handle the daily tasks of working with Search and Rescue.

This night was much like all the others. After her shift ended, Finley usually went to *Oasis*, a small watering hole down the road from the Merritt Island Airport, where the Coast Guard Air Station was located. She'd been stationed at Merritt Island for close to three years now, and three years was the magic number for your name to come up on transfer. She'd rented a little bungalow, close to the Banana River and only a mile from the base, when she'd first moved there. The cost was higher, but she was sick of renting dingy, little apartments. This would mean she'd have to give notice to the home owner in a few months just to be sure she could break her lease before her transfer came up—something she was expecting to happen in mid

December.

She'd started out in Savannah, Georgia for the first three years after completing boot camp, the Aviation Survival Technician training program (A-School), to become a Rescue Swimmer, as well as the EMT training that went along with it. Since the Coast Guard was broken up into districts covering a group of states, whatever district you were given out of boot camp was pretty much the area of the country you would remain in throughout your career. Every district was broken up into air stations and marine units that were scattered around.

After Savannah, Finley's next assignment was Clearwater, Florida for three years. After that she was transferred to Air Station San Juan, Puerto Rico, which was also part of her district.

Now, she was back in Florida at Coast Guard Air Station Merritt Island, which wasn't far from Cape Canaveral and Cocoa Beach. She was happy with her life in the Coast Guard. A routine day was never a possibility, but that's what kept the job interesting. She found herself making some of the most daring rescues at sea over the years, with several of those coming on a daily basis during the summer months. She was thirty-one, and after thirteen years of service, she'd worked her way up to the rank of Chief Petty Officer. She planned on staying in until she could retire after twenty years. The money wasn't bad, and it wasn't like she had a life to come home to. She was single in every shape of the word and definitely not looking to change her status. Most of the personnel knew she was a lesbian. A couple of other flight crew members were as well, but none of that mattered when you depended on each other day in and day out to work as a team while risking your own life to save others.

*

The *Oasis* wasn't overly crowded for a Wednesday night. Finley sipped a light beer and watched a few sailors from Cape Canaveral Naval Base who were dancing on the hardwood floor. During her time at Merritt Island, she'd seen a number of fights in the bar. The Coast Guard and Navy tended to get into heated discussions when too much alcohol was involved, but most of the time everyone simply mixed together and had a good time.

Greg Ballard and Tracy Pollack, two of her good friends, whom she also served on aircrews with, were sitting at the small, round table with her. Greg was a lieutenant and a pilot for the Sikorsky MH65-Dolphin, the helicopters they used at Merritt Island. Tracey was an Aviation Maintenance Technician Second Class and a Flight Mechanic.

"Why do we come here?" Greg asked with a sigh as he finished the last of his watered down soda.

"Because there is nowhere else to go," Tracy answered him truthfully.

There really wasn't anywhere else to go unless you wanted to hang out with the tourists or go on the mainland. Finley didn't mind. She'd spent many nights in some sort of military bar at various stages in her career.

"How is your hand, Finley?" Greg asked, glancing down at her left hand.

"Fine. It stopped hurting by the time we were back on base." She shrugged. One of the Aviation Maintenance Technicians who was training to be a Flight Mechanic, misunderstood the direction she gave him earlier that day when they were trying to wrangle a passenger from a distressed boat. What should have been a routine rescue on a clear day, turned ugly when the young AMT accidentally reversed the cable on the hoist, causing the rescue basket to go out of control. Finley's fingers got smashed between the helicopter and the basket. If she hadn't been there to catch the basket, it would've plummeted back down into the water with the man stuck inside of it. Once they got the man out and attended to him, Finley shoved the AMT against the wall inside the helicopter, threatening to hang him on the cable by his balls if he ever made that mistake again. Luckily, her hand was only bruised instead of broken.

"I couldn't believe he pushed the release on the hoist. Shit. If you had fallen out, it would've killed you, not to mention the dude in the basket."

"Trust me, I don't think he'll be flying with any of us again," Tracy said. "I heard him asking for a transfer to fixed wing."

All three of them laughed.

"I may have scared him a little," Finley admitted.

"You? I guess when you're commanding an operation you can be a little intimidating, but you save lives and you do it safely. Everyone respects you out there." Greg smiled. "But we all know your secrets back on the ground," he kidded.

"Oh please," she chuckled. "I have secrets that would make you grow hair!"

"Hey, don't knock the bald guy." He tried faking a frown.

"I'm so glad I have the next two days off!" Tracey cheered, raising her glass.

"Me too, but I'm on standby and will probably get called in," Greg added.

4

Finley smiled and shook her head. The aircrews rotated in twelve-hour shifts, with two days, or forty-eight hours off after every twenty-four hours of duty. They either worked from seven a.m. to seven p.m., which was the day shift, or seven p.m. to seven a.m., which was the night shift, alternating every three weeks. During the forty-eight hours off, part of the aircrew members were on standby in case of emergency. The standby schedule varied week to week.

*

It was close to ten o'clock by the time Finley made it back to her small house. She parked her Explorer in the single car driveway and meandered inside. She needed to be up at five in order to be on the base and inside the hangar in time for the seven a.m. shift change. Her rotation schedule was a day off of Greg and Tracey's because she'd been called in twice during her last standby time off.

She walked into the carpeted living room that was decorated with light-colored wood furniture, and a matching sand-colored, leather couch and love seat. There was a stone fireplace in the corner of the room and an abundance of pictures across the mantel. Finley noticed a light blinking on the phone when she turned the corner to go towards her bedroom. She hesitated, wondering who would've called her landline. She'd had her cell phone with her and it never rang all day. The only people with her home phone number were her family and the base in case she was called in for an emergency and they couldn't reach her on the cell. She pressed the button and sat on the edge of the couch, listening to the message.

"Finley, it's Nicole –"

That voice was all she needed to hear to send her

mind back tumbling back in time.

*

It was a few months into their senior year of high school at Annandale High in Charleston, South Carolina. Finley and Nicole "Nic" Wetherby were looking forward to graduating at the end of the year. They were best friends, completely inseparable since their freshman year, after they nearly knocked each other over in the hallway, running late for the same class. Nicole had honey blond hair that hung just past the top of her shoulders and hazel eyes. She was three inches shorter than Finley and had a slender build with curves in all the right places. If the guys weren't asking her out, they were chasing after Finley, who was tall and very athletic with curly, dark hair and big blue eyes. Finley knew she had feelings for Nicole, feelings that she was supposed to be having for the boys, but she kept them a secret, and buried it deep inside.

"I think we should go to Daniel's party this weekend." Nicole was sitting behind Finley, playing in her hair. She loved the soft, natural curls and spent countless hours running her fingers through them while they contemplated ideas of their future.

"Oh, I don't know, Nic." Finley wasn't much for parties and guys hanging all over her. Plus, she absolutely hated watching her older brother, Michael, swoon all over Nicole. He was a year ahead of them and already attending the local community college. He had no goals, not even possibilities. But, Jackie Morris, Finley and Michael's mother, had made it very clear that he'd either go to college or move out. She wasn't supporting him if he wasn't working on a college degree in something. She was a school teacher who ruled the house with an iron fist, but she was never abusive towards her children. She simply wanted to see them make something of themselves, instead of working various jobs, sometimes more than one at a time, to make ends meet. Their father had left right after Finley was born, and he never returned. Jackie Morris said good riddance to the man and had never looked back. Of course, she struggled from time to time like any single mother who was trying to feed her kids and pay a mortgage on a meager teacher's salary, but her two kids never went hungry and always had decent clothing. Both of her children were extremely smart. However, Michael had spent his time playing around and barely graduated. Whereas Finley was an honor student and a major athlete. She'd won multiple awards on the swim team and had been the captain for the last three years. The track coach had tried to recruit her because he'd seen her running as part of her extra cardio fitness on multiple occasions. Her times were fairly good, but the only thing that had appealed to her was swimming.

"Come on, Fin. Mike wants me to go with him, but I'd rather go with you, and then see him there." Nicole didn't date many guys. She'd rather spend her time hanging out with Finley, which was fine with Finley since she didn't date guys at all. She always put it off to school and swimming, saying she didn't have time to date and wasn't interested in teenage boys when she'd be in college soon, where she'd have the pick of the litter.

Finley found it impossible to argue with Nicole, especially when she was playing in her hair. Hell, she could barely form a sentence. "Fine. But, I'm not drinking and then driving us home. You know Mike will be hammered, he always is at parties."

"I know. We don't have to drink. I just want to go

see what all of the fuss is about. I hear Daniel throws a kickass party," Nicole said with pouty eyes. "Come on. I won't go without you."

The night of the party Finley saw Mike stumbling around looking for Nicole. What she didn't realize was he had already found her an hour earlier, convincing her to lose her virginity since he was a college guy and wouldn't play games with her like the high school boys. Of course, his crappy lines worked after she'd had a few drinks.

"Where's Nicole?" he asked, his speech slightly slurred.

"I saw her talking to you a while ago. Come to think of it, I haven't seen her since," she answered.

Mike looked upset and this made Finley nervous, so she wandered around until she found Nicole sitting on the hood of Finley's old, blue Honda Civic at the end of the road.

"What's wrong, Nic?" Finley asked. When she saw the tears in Nicole's golden green eyes, she hopped up on the hood next to her, wrapping her arms around her best friend. "Tell me."

"I...oh, Finley,...I made a huge mistake. How could..." She sniffled and wiped the falling tears from her face. "I am so stupid."

"No you're not. What happened?" Finley held Nicole and let her cry until she could finally talk again.

"Can you take me home now?"

"Sure."

On the way to Nicole's house, she broke down and told Finley about sleeping with Mike. She'd said she only did it to look cool, but felt horrible about it afterwards. She wished over and over that she could take it all back. Finley did the only thing a best friend could do, she consoled her and told her it would be okay. She also said she never had to do it again if she didn't want to.

Three hours later, Finley was asleep in her own bed when her mom came barging into the room, screaming. Finley flew out of the bed thinking the house was on fire. Either that, or something had happened to Nicole. Since she hadn't heard from her after she'd dropped her off earlier and came home. Maybe her parents had found out what she'd done.

"Your brother..." That was all Jackie Morris could get out. She was hysterical.

"What? What did Mike do now? Where is he?" Finley moved passed her mom and into her brother's room. It was empty. She proceeded down the hallway and into the living room. That's where she found the male police officer standing just inside the front door.

"What are you doing here?" Finley had completely forgotten she was wearing a tiny little tank top and shorts with nothing underneath. The man quickly turned his eyes to the floor.

"I'm Officer Harvey. Is Mrs. Morris okay?" he asked with a deep voice.

"She's flipping out. What the hell is going on?" Finley was almost eye-level with the officer since she wasn't much shorter than him.

"There's been an accident. Michael Morris's car ran the stop light on Gilcrest and Seventh, and an oncoming car hit his, causing it to flip a couple of times and land upside down."

"Where is he? What hospital?" she asked, cutting him off as she mentally listed what she needed to do. She had to get her mother calmed down and head to the hospital immediately.

"I'm sorry, he didn't make it. Michael Morris died at the scene of the accident before they could get him out of the car."

"What? No! Oh God!" Finley screamed Michael's name and swore.

"I'm very sorry," the Officer said. "He had his license with him, but I need someone to make an ID at the hospital."

Finley was shaking so badly, she could hardly stand up. She knew her mother was in her brother's room and in no shape to go see his dead body. She wasn't either for that matter. "I'll go," she murmured before walking back up the stairs to change her clothes. On the way out, she ran over to Mrs. Cooley's house next door and explained to her what happened so she could come sit with her mom.

*

Finley continued to hold the pause button on the phone. Standing there in her house some fourteen years later, she could still smell the hospital stench of bleach mixed with the metallic tinge of blood as she walked through the trauma department behind the officer. She didn't have to close her eyes to remember the sight behind the curtain to the left. A thin white sheet had covered her brother's lifeless body. When the doctor pulled it back, she looked down at his face. It was cut up from the broken glass and caked with dried blood. He hadn't had his seat belt on, but surprisingly, he hadn't gone through the windshield. The doctor had told Finley that his blood alcohol level was three times the legal limit and he'd died of a massive head trauma.

Finley rubbed her throbbing temple with her free

hand and let go of the button on the phone after restarting the message. She held her breath as she listened to a voice she hadn't heard in seven years.

"Finley, it's Nicole. You need to be at the airport tomorrow at eight p.m. Your daughter is coming to stay the last few weeks of her summer break with you," she said in a soft voice. Then there was a sigh and a click as the phone was hung up.

"What!" Finley jumped and replayed the message again. "Son of a bitch, Nicole."

Chapter 2

Finley sat down on the couch with her elbows on her knees and her head in her hands. Her mind drifted back to high school once more. Her brother's funeral passed and the world had finally started to settle down again. Over the next six weeks, Finley was pulled in so many directions she didn't know which way was up anymore. That's when Nicole asked if she could stay the night one Friday so they could finally have time to grieve together. Nicole had been the only thing keeping her grounded.

"I'm glad you came over. We've had no time to just sit and talk since the accident." Nicole sat on Finley's bed next to her and grabbed both of her hands, pulling them into her lap. "We both lost something that night. He was your brother, but he was also my friend. I didn't love him, but I cared for him enough to have sex with him for the first time. I know I was stupid, and it was a very stupid thing to do, but I think it happened for a reason."

"What? Why would you say that? There is no reason why my brother should have died. I tried to tell him to slow down and pace himself, but I was the 'little sister.' What the hell did I know? Well, I know one thing, I'm alive because I wasn't as careless as he was, and I never will be."

"I know. That's what I love about you, Finley. You're so damn smart. I should've listened to you. Everything would be different if I had just listened to you."

"What do you mean?" Finley raised an eyebrow and met Nicole's sparkling eyes.

"I'm pregnant," she whispered.

"No. Oh, Nic." Finley wrapped her arms around Nicole and pulled her tightly against her chest. They sat like that for minutes that felt like hours. "Does your family know?"

"Yeah. I tried to tell them it was only that one night, but my mom and dad don't believe me. They are so pissed off, they threatened to send me away and make me have an abortion. Luckily, my mom is too damn right-winged and religious for that."

"I'll be here for you, Nic. Whatever you want or need I'll do it. We can still move in together like we planned and get jobs after graduation. We can both go to college too."

"I don't know what I'm going to do. My mom has already told me she's not helping me support this baby. She keeps calling it 'the mistake'."

Finley felt Nicole's warm tears soaking her shirt collar. She tried not to let her feelings surface, but she had no choice. She pulled back slightly, looking into Nicole's eyes before she closed the distance, kissing her softly.

Nicole froze and pulled away. She stared up into Finley's deep blue eyes. Her hand quivered as she brought it up to meet Finley's face. She pulled Finley back towards her until their lips met again, soft at first. Then their lips parted, allowing their tongues to explore each other. This was a whole new feeling for Finley and an awakening for Nicole.

*

The day of their high school graduation, Finley pulled Nicole to the side and opened an envelope, showing her the contents.

"Where the hell did you get that?" Nicole squeaked, looking at the cash bills with bug eyes.

"You know I've been working at the sporting goods store since before Christmas. This is all of my paychecks, plus the money my family sent me for graduation. It's only about five thousand dollars, but it's enough for an apartment, plus furniture and household bills. I want you to move in with me. We can do this baby thing together, you and me."

"What are you saying, Finley?"

"Nicole–" Finley put the envelope back in her pocket and pulled Nicole further behind the bushes. She'd never called her by her first name unless it was serious or she was mad. "This isn't just some fling or experiment for me. I..." she paused, trying to calm her racing heart. "I'm in love with you. I've been in love with you since our sophomore year. I've wanted to say that to you so many times."

Nicole closed the distance between them, standing on her toes to kiss Finley's lips in a lingering kiss that ended when they heard voices close by.

"Finley, I...I don't know what to say."

"Say you'll spend the rest of your life with me," Finley murmured as a tear rolled down her cheek.

Nicole wrapped her arms around Finley's neck, kissing her again. Her round belly pushed against Finley's midsection. This time there was no stopping because of the voices. Nicole threaded her fingers into Finley's dark, curly hair, kissing her with as much heated passion as she possibly could. They pulled away from each other breathlessly.

"I love you too, Finley. I always have and always will. You're my best friend and the love of my life."

Finley couldn't wipe the smile from her face if she wanted to.

"I think we should start apartment hunting today." Nicole grinned.

*

A week later, they'd moved into a tiny, two bedroom apartment and signed a one year lease. Then, they bought minimal living room and bedroom furniture, plus a crib and dresser set for the baby's room.

"Are you sure it's only for eight weeks? I don't know if I can be away from you for eight whole weeks," Nicole said. She'd pleaded with Finley to change her mind after she told her she'd enlisted in the Coast Guard. Nicole knew Finley didn't want a 'job'. She wanted to be 'something,' and she had the drive to do whatever she wanted to do. She loved swimming and the best place to put her talent to work, making a difference, was with the Coast Guard as a Rescue Swimmer. She had planned to take the swimming scholarship that was offered to her and go to college, but with Nicole there and the baby on the way, she needed an income, not a degree. The Coast Guard would provide her with a career, a steady income with health insurance, and a retirement plan if she stayed in long enough.

Nicole had gotten a job as a bank receptionist and was taking college classes at night, while Finley trained rigorously before she had to leave for boot camp. Because of her strong swimming skills and high test scores, she was accepted to Aviation Survival Technician school and Helicopter Rescue Swimmer training, which was twenty-four weeks long, plus seven weeks of EMT training after that. The baby wasn't due for another ten weeks. She prayed to God that she was there for the birth, and that it happened during the two weeks she'd be home between boot camp and AST school. After that, she'd be stationed somewhere and spend the next six months working on her qualifications, before moving on to finish Rescue Swimmer school.

"Nic, you'll be fine. I'm going to miss you like crazy though."

"Oh yeah, how much?" Nicole teased.

Finley laid her back on the bed and scooted up beside her.

"Why don't I show you?" She wiggled her eyebrows, placing soft kisses along Nicole's collarbone and across her chest as she removed her clothing one piece at a time. Nicole slowly helped Finley out of her own clothes until they were lying naked on the bed, wrapped in each other's arms.

"You drive me insane," Nicole said breathlessly. "I've never wanted anything as much as I want you."

"I know, I can't get enough of you either." Finley flicked her tongue over both enlarged nipples as she worked her way down, carefully kissing Nicole's large, round belly. She knew better than to go any further with her kisses. Nicole wanted to see her and she couldn't with her belly protruding, so Finley promised not to disappear until after the baby was born. Nicole was a passionate lover. One that liked to hold and be held as they were making love. Finley gave her whole heart to Nicole over and over again every time they were intimate with each other.

"I love you," Nicole said as she felt Finley's finger's slide through her wetness and enter her gently. "You make me feel like I've never felt before."

"I love you too. I always have," Finley whispered as she nibbled her ear and worked her fingers in and out slowly, increasing when she felt Nicole's hips rise to meet her hand. She pressed her thumb against her throbbing clit and moved it in circles, matching the pressure of her fingers. Nicole's body tightened around Finley's fingers, pulling them further inside.

"Yes...Oh, Finley,...you feel so good!" Nicole grabbed Finley, holding her tightly until the last of the orgasm washed over her.

Their lovemaking lasted a little while longer, following them into the shower as Nicole took over Finley's muscled body, nearly bringing her to her knees with simple touches.

*

Finley stilled her thoughts long enough to get a grip on reality. What the hell was she going to do with a teenage kid living with her?

She smiled when she thought back to the day Nicole's baby was born. She'd only been home from boot camp a week, and luckily had one more week to go before she'd have to leave for twenty-four weeks of AST school. Even though she'd basically be in the same town since the school was also in Charleston, she'd be confined to the base for the majority of the time there.

They'd rushed to the hospital when Nicole's water broke in the kitchen of their apartment. Finley's mother had been the first to arrive behind them. Nicole's mother had arrived just after her. The two of them sat apart from each other in the waiting room to keep from arguing. Barbara Wetherby swore Michael Morris wasn't the only guy her daughter had slept with, and she was certain he wasn't the father of the baby.

Finley was in the room, holding Nicole's hand when a head full of dark, curly hair popped out. Seconds later, the rest of the tiny baby girl came out, kicking and screaming. She had the biggest blue eyes.

Nicole turned towards Finley. "She looks just like you! Oh, my God," she cried as tears stung her eyes.

Michael had looked a lot like Finley in the face, but his dark hair wasn't curly, and his eyes weren't blue, they were brown. Finley had inherited her looks from their long lost father. Finley cried when Nicole handed her the warm bundle. The baby squeezed Finley's finger with her whole hand and made tiny little noises.

"She loves you, just like I do," Nicole whispered.

"I love you," Finley replied, leaning over to kiss Nicole's sweaty cheek. "And I will love her like she's my own for the rest of my life."

"She *is* yours, Finley. She may never have a father, but this baby girl will always have two mothers," Nicole said through thick tears. Even though Finley had already given blood, and the doctors would test the baby's blood against her own to prove Michael's paternity, it was unmistakably clear this baby shared Finley's genes.

"What are you ladies going to name her?" the nurse asked as she stepped over to them with the birth certificate.

Nicole looked at Finley and smiled. "Caitlin Finley Morris."

"Nic!" Finley's eyes grew wide.

Nicole squeezed her hand and winked at her.

"You'll never be able to deny her now, Finley. She's going to love you as much as I do, I just know it."

"I'd never deny her, or you."

*

Finley felt a tear slip from her eye and wet her cheek as it slid down. That day, thirteen years ago, was the greatest day of her life, next to the first time Nicole had told her she loved her. "I'm not ready for this. Thanks a fucking lot, Nic. You can't just put her on a plane and send her down to me: no warning, no reason, no fucking nothing." She wanted to call Nic and let her have it, but hearing her voice over the machine was achingly painful enough.

*

The next morning, Finley dressed in her operational daily uniform, a sage green-colored flight suit with a dark blue t-shirt and shorts under it, and black flight boots. The upper left chest of the flight suit had a black, rectangle patch with her first and last name on it in gold letters. The Aviation Rescue Swimmer insignia: a pair of gold aviation wings with the EMT star of life in the center and a pair of swim fins crossed over it, was embroidered above her name. Rescue Swimmer was written below her name. The upper right chest had a white, rectangle United States Coast Guard patch. An American flag patch was on the outside of the upper left arm. The opposite arm had a circular patch with USCG Air Station Merritt Island written around the circle, and in the center was an orange HT-65 Dolphin helicopter. Rescue was written above the helo with Swimmer written below it. Finley rolled the long sleeves of the flight suit up three-quarters of the way, and finished the ensemble with dark blue baseball cap that had US Coast Guard Station Merritt Island stitched in gold with her Chief Petty Officer rank insignia in the middle.

During the short drive to the base, Finley's mind replayed the message from the prior evening. She was mad at Nicole for literally dumping their daughter on her without warning, but she was also excited at the chance to spend time with her since she was only able to visit her a few times a year.

*

"Good morning. How's your hand? I heard you smashed it pretty good," Command Master Chief George Newberry asked. He was standing in the main hangar of the air station.

"It's fine." She flexed it a few times to show him.

He nodded, stepping inside his office, and motioning for her to follow. "Have you given anymore thought to my offer? The captain is ready to give you a glowing recommendation," he said. As the assistant to the captain of the base, his job was in administration, and more importantly, personnel. He handled all incoming and outgoing transfer orders, on top of other duties.

Finley held her breath. Less than twenty-four hours earlier, she'd been offered an instructor position at the rescue swimmer school in Charleston. The same one she'd attended. It was a three year post like any other base assignment. She just wasn't sure she wanted to get off the front lines for that long, much less, be that close to Nicole. The thought of being closer to Caitlin was the only reason she was even contemplating the idea.

"I know it's a tough decision. Taking you out of the field is going to hurt District 7, but you're one of the best rescue swimmers I've ever seen. Having you as an instructor for the next three years could impact so many rookies. You were there once. I'm sure you have one or two instructors that stand out in your mind to this day that taught you something valuable."

Finley nodded.

"If you do it for a year and completely hate it, you can ask for a transfer or reassignment. In three years time, you'd be back in the water, doing what you do best. Hell, do the three years at the school, then another three year post and you'll probably make senior chief before you turn forty. That's a rarity in and of itself."

"I know. I'm still thinking about it," she finally said.

"You still have a few months. Your post here isn't up until the end of December."

Finley nodded again. She had less than six months. Thinking about the summer, she remembered why she was there and quickly left his office. Down the hall, near the dispatch office, was the office of the Operations Duty Officer. The ODO handled the duty operations for each shift, as well as all of the scheduling. She knocked on the door and walked inside.

"Morris, you're not supposed to be on shift for at least a half hour," Commander Robert Douglas stated. "Is your hand okay?"

"It's fine. I know I need to put in for personal time sixty days ahead, but I was just made aware last night that my daughter is flying down to stay a few weeks with me during her summer break. I was hoping we could adjust my rotation so I can be on standby this weekend instead of active. I'll need a little time to get her settled in," Finley said, twisting her ball cap in her hand.

The tall, broad-shouldered man standing in front of her ran a hand over his bald head. "I didn't know you had children, Morris."

"She's thirteen and lives in Charleston," she replied.

"Wow," he murmured, raising an eyebrow. He'd never seen Finley at any of the family events on base and was completely unaware. "Charleston…that should be a sign." He grinned.

Finley ignored him. "I only get to see her a few times a year, and that is usually when I travel up there. So, I have a lot of preparation to do with her coming to stay with me."

"I see. When does she arrive?" he questioned.

"This evening."

He smiled, knowing how hard it was to take care of a teenager himself. "You don't have much time then."

"No," she murmured.

"Take liberty tomorrow and I'll push you to the back of the rotation. This will give you Friday off, with Saturday and Sunday on call," he said, looking at the large dry-erase board on the wall with the aircrew schedule written on it.

"Thank you," she said before stepping out of his office and heading across the hangar to do her paperwork for the morning shift change.

Chapter 3

Finley parked her Explorer in the waiting lot and walked inside the airport terminal. She hadn't seen Caitlin in about six months, but she could spot the child in any crowd. Plus, she had pictures of her in various stages of her life plastered across her fireplace mantel.

The woman standing behind the ticket counter waved for the next person, and the man in front of Finley told her to go ahead. Finley was still wearing her flight suit, but had taken her ball cap off.

"Can I help you ma'am?"

"Yes, my thirteen year old daughter is coming in on flight eight-twelve from Charleston," Finley answered, showing her military ID.

"No problem. I'll call security to take you down to her gate. It looks like the plane is on time and scheduled to arrive in about ten minutes."

"Thanks." Finley stepped to the side and waited for the Homeland Security Guard to walk her through the scanners at the security check.

"Hello, ma'am. If you'll follow me, I'll take you to gate B-6 to meet your daughter's plane. You should be able to walk through the scanner in your flight suit. If not, we'll scan you with a wand," he said. After 9/11 the entire country had gone crazy over travel security. The airports had become extremely difficult to navigate through as a ticketed passenger, and it was impossible to go anywhere near the gates if you didn't have a ticket.

Finley remembered back about nine years ago when you could meet your party at their arriving gate. Nicole had taken Caitlin to the airport to pick her up when she returned from advanced training in Connecticut. Finley let her mind drift back to that time.

*

It wasn't long after Finley's return from her three weeks of advanced training, when her relationship began to take a turn for the worse. Baby Caitlin was now five years old, and they were living in Clearwater, Florida. Finley had been transferred there after her first three years in Savannah. The Coast Guard had turned out to be a perfect fit for Finley. She loved being a Helicopter Rescue Swimmer. Nicole was working as a bank teller during the day, and doing online classes for her bachelor's degree at night. She had about two and a half months left before she'd graduate.

While Finley was away training, Nicole's mother made a surprise visit to Clearwater to try and talk some sense into her daughter. Nicole had refused to hear what she had to say at first, but eventually she'd listened to the preaching, and saw the hurt in her mother's eyes when she talked about Nicole's father being sick with cancer. She also went on and on about Finley having to move every three years and how it wasn't fair to Nicole or Caitlin to have to pick up everything to follow her.

"Mom visited while you were gone."

"Did you tell her to fuck off?"

"Finley! She's my mother for God's sake."

24

"What did she want this time, Nic? What could she possibly have to say so bad that she came to Florida?"

"My father has cancer."

"We both know that. We went home and visited them last year."

"He's dying."

"I'm sorry, Nic, but that woman would use anything to get you away from me."

"What happens when you get shipped off again in six months and my father dies?"

"What do you want me to say? You know I have to go where they tell me, Nic. I'm in the military. The Coast Guard has given us a pretty decent life, and you've never had a problem moving before."

"Well, my father wasn't sick before. I just don't know if I can do it, Finley. I'm thinking of taking Caitlin back home when you move again."

"Nicole! What are you talking about? We love each other. We're happy together. I don't understand."

"I want to spend time with him before he dies. I want Caitlin to know her grandpa. I love you, Finley, and I always will, but I can't keep following you all over because you joined the military. This is your lifestyle, not mine."

Nicole and Caitlin were gone three months later.

*

Finley was standing to the side, watching the men and women walk by as they debarked the plane. She almost missed the young girl walking by her. She looked too tall and athletic to be a thirteen year old kid, but the dark, curly hair and blue eyes were unmistakable.

"Hey, Mom!" Caitlin said, throwing her arms

25

around Finley's neck. Caitlin was almost as tall as Finley remembered Nicole being.

"Oh, my God! Caitlin, you've grown a foot since the last time I saw you." Finley wrapped her arms around her daughter, holding her as long as the girl would allow. Caitlin finally pulled away with a thin frown on her face.

"It has been a while since you've seen me, I guess." Caitlin finally grinned sheepishly. "I'm as tall as Mom now. I'll be able to see over her head like you can, soon." She took this as a major accomplishment. All girls wanted to be taller than their mother. It was a superiority complex for a teenager.

Finley felt the tug on her heart when Caitlin referenced her lack of visits, but she laughed when Caitlin cheered up after thinking about outgrowing her mom. *God, she looks so much like the Morris's.* "Well, come on, kiddo. I'm sure you have more than just that little bag there. I know how your mom packs, and it's definitely not light."

"Yeah, no kidding. I bet you could fit your entire wardrobe in this bag." She pointed to the small carry-on suitcase she was wheeling along behind her as they walked towards the baggage claim area.

Finley glanced down at the bag and bit her bottom lip. "I could, but the military teaches you that on the first day when they make you throw away everything you brought with you." She smiled thinking back to her first day of boot camp. She thought she'd die before the day was even over, but somehow she'd survived.

"I've never seen you in your flight suit, unless you count the old pictures Mom has of you when you were younger." Caitlin studied the patches on the drab-green, zip up suit.

"I'm not working when I come up to see you."

Finley smiled. *She'd flip out if she saw all of the crap hanging off of my Service Dress Blue uniform.*

*

They retrieved two large suitcases and made their way towards the SUV. Finley couldn't believe her eyes. Here was her little girl, all grown up, and she'd missed most of that. Two or three visits a year was the biggest mistake she'd ever made. She was seeing that with her own eyes like a slap in the face. She silently prayed that Caitlin understood why she stayed away.

"So, Mom didn't tell me much about where you live. She just said in Florida. You never talk much about it either."

"Well, that's probably because I move every three years," Finley sighed. "I have a house by the river inlet and my air station is close to Port Canaveral, where NASA's Kennedy Space Center is."

"No way! Can we go there?"

"Sure." Finley smiled, glancing at her. "So—" she started, then paused to take a deep breath as she pulled out onto the main road. "Your mom didn't say much about your visit for the summer when she called."

"I'm sure she just left you a message. She's a coward!" Caitlin huffed.

"Caitlin! That is no way to talk about your mother," Finley growled. The kid was right, Nicole was a coward, but Finley couldn't let her be disrespectful.

"Well, she is." Caitlin stared out the window at the passing cars.

Finley sensed a subject change and decided this wasn't the time to have this discussion. She'd wait until Caitlin was settled in.

27

After a quick stop for pizza, they made it to the house. Finley loved her quaint, cozy little bungalow, but living with someone was something she hadn't done since Nicole left her. It was definitely going to take some getting used to.

"I like your house. It's cute," Caitlin said as she took her bags to her room and began to unpack.

Finley set out plates for the pizza, and changed into a pair of cotton shorts and a t-shirt. She still couldn't get over how much Caitlin resembled her. It was like looking at her teenage self with the attitude to go with it.

"Go ahead and call your mom so she knows you arrived safely," Finley said, stepping out of her bedroom. She hadn't spoken to Nicole in years. They simply kept in touch for Caitlin's sake through short emails, and Finley's mother ran interference for the visits. Nicole also had Caitlin send holiday and birthday cards with school pictures in them.

Finley started on her plate of pizza at the dining room table while Caitlin sat on the couch in the nearby living room, talking to her mother. Finley heard Caitlin saying she had arrived and Mom was taking her to see NASA. After a long pause the excitement in Caitlin's voice was gone as she huffed 'yes ma'am'. Then in a monotone voice, 'hi Dave, yes, uh huh, no, the flight was okay.' After that, she hung up. Finley felt her jaw clinch when she heard his name. Her appetite was lost as her mind scrolled through a memory she wished she could erase.

Nicole and Caitlin had been living back in Charleston for nearly three years when Finley received a letter saying Nicole had met someone. A man no doubt. His name was David Dulinberg. He was a Jewish man in his early forties, much older than Nicole, and a friend of her father's from the golf league he was on. Finley was so severely sick to her stomach after that, she was put on the no fly list for the rest of the week.

The next letter came three months later.

Finley,
These are Caitlin's class pictures and pictures from her field trip to the old fort. She keeps asking when you're going to visit. I'll help her call you next week. I want you to send her presents to her early this year, and please put them in Hanukkah paper. Dave's Jewish and we're celebrating with him this year. Also, Dave and I are planning on getting married after the first of the year. I don't expect you to be there, but I'll send you an invitation anyway.
Nicole

Finley balled the letter up and threw it in the trash can after she ran to the bathroom and puked until there was nothing left. Then, she got it out of the trash and tore it to pieces and threw it away again. Then, she didn't want it in her house, so she took the trash to the road. She was barely back in the house when she decided she didn't want it anywhere near her. Therefore, she grabbed her keys and tossed the bag in the trunk of her car, driving it in the nearest dumpster. She didn't have to worry about rereading the letter, every word was burned into her memory. She took the love that she still held for Nicole and turned it into hatred. She was living on base since she was stationed in Puerto Rico, so she went for a run down on the docks where the marine fleet was located.

Three months later another letter came, along with the dreaded invitation. Finley never opened the invitation, instead she tossed it out of the helicopter that night. She had done the same thing after reading the letter asking for Finley's permission to allow Dave to adopt her. Once she calmed down enough to talk, Finley called her mother and told her what Nicole's plans were. Then, she dialed one more number.

"Hello?" A man's voice answered.

"Is Nicole Wetherby there?" Finley's tone was flat. She had nothing left. She'd been throwing up for days, not eating and not sleeping. She'd lost almost ten pounds in a week. Her Operations Duty Officer threatened to pull her off of duty. She had to go through the rounds with the doctors until they finally said it was a flu bug and gave her antibiotics. She knew she had better straighten up or she was going to flush her career down the toilet.

"Yes she is. May I ask who's calling?"

"No. Just put Nicole on the phone." I don't have time for your bullshit, dickhead.

"Hello? This is Nicole."

"What the hell do you think you're doing, Nic? Have you lost your god damn mind?!" Finley's tone was threatening.

"Finley, calm down."

"If you want to lie around with some man playing house, that's your problem. I'll never forgive you for putting me through this, Nicole, but you're not dragging my daughter into your sick, twisted fuck-up. Do you hear me! That child is and always will be a Morris! My blood, Nicole! My god damn blood! Not his!" She was yelling so loud, Nicole had to leave the room so that Dave didn't overhear her conversation.

"Stop yelling at me, Finley!" Nicole did her best to fight back.

"*I swear to God, Nicole. I'll come up there and we can do this face to face. It's your call.*"

"*No, you don't need to come up here to fight with me. Dave's a nice guy. He's good with Caitlin.*"

"*I don't give a shit if he's fucking Saint Christian himself. He's not raising her like she's his. You took her from me, you wrecked my life, Nicole. I'll be damned if I'm going to sit back and watch you push me completely out of her life!*"

"*I'd never do that. You and your mother are her family too.*"

"*You're damn right we are.*"

"*What's with your language? I don't like hearing it.*"

"*Too fucking bad. You've pissed me off to the point of no return this time,*" Finley growled. "*Oh, and how's your father? I hear he's still alive and playing golf every day.*"

"*That's not fair, Finley. He's still sick.*"

"*Uh huh. I'm sure Barbara is playing that fiddle over and over.*"

"*What?*"

"*Never mind. I mean it, Nicole. You change her last name and so help me, I'll be on your doorstep before you teach her how to spell it. You understand?*"

"*Yes. I'm sorry. I...I never should have—*"

"*You're damn right you shouldn't have. I can't believe you're so fucking gullible. I bet your mom's had the wedding planned since before you even met him.*"

*

"Ugh!" Caitlin huffed in frustration as she made her

way back into the kitchen.

"Everything okay?" Finley asked as she slid the pizza box over to her.

"Mom's just getting on my nerves."

"Oh."

"She expects me to just bend over and kiss Dave's as…uh…" Caitlin's blue eyes grew large when she looked up to meet the same eyes staring back at her behind raised brows and a half eaten slice of pizza. "I'm sorry," she squeaked.

"You're damn right you are." Finley felt the muscle in her jaw clinch. "There won't be swearing in my house."

"But, you just swore," Caitlin chided.

"Caitlin Finley Morris, I am an adult. When you turn eighteen, you can cuss me out if you want, but until then you will respect adults."

"Don't tell me you're just like her. I'm not going to be nice to that man, and you're not going to make me either." Caitlin jumped up and stormed off to her room. Finley started after her, but decided to wait and find out the real story behind the anger and frustration causing the kid to lash out.

"So help me, Nic. If he's laid a hand on my little girl, I'll kill you both," she whispered to herself.

Chapter 4

Finley let another day go by before calling Nicole to find out just exactly when their daughter had developed the attitude from hell. Caitlin had been short with her anytime she'd asked about home. She didn't have much to say about school either. She was heading into high school at the end of the summer and had already chosen her classes for her freshman year. She was set to attend the same high school that Finley and Nicole had graduated from. Finley knew this could be a very stressful time in Caitlin's life, but it should also be a very happy time for her. Most children looked forward to high school.

"Hello?" a sweet, almost innocent voice answered the phone on the second ring.

Even after all of the years and the turmoil between them, Finley still felt her breath catch in her throat.

"Nic, it's Finley."

Silence followed.

"Is Caitlin okay?" Nicole asked.

"What the hell is going on? You don't speak to me for years. You force me to communicate with my daughter away from you. Then, out of the blue, you put her on a plane and ship her to me without so much as a warning, or a hello, or even a fuck you."

"Finley!"

"I'm serious, Nic. What's going on with her? She's

definitely upset about something and you're hiding it from me. You obviously sent her here because the two of you aren't getting along. What's the deal?"

Another long silence only made matters worse. Finley huffed in frustration.

Nicole sighed. "Dave just got home from work. Can I call you back when he goes to bed?"

"Fine." Finley pushed the button to end the call, wishing she could toss her cell phone against the wall as she poured herself a glass of single malt. She needed it to get through her first real conversation with Nicole in almost seven years. She was still shaking from the nervousness of that initial call. Some of the alcohol splashed onto the table. *Damn it, Finley, get it together. Stop letting that woman get to you!*

*

Finley was leaning over the open door of the H65-Dolphin, peering down at the water as they flew over the Atlantic Ocean, searching for a boat that had been missing since a mayday call was received early that day. She stifled a yawn, wishing she'd drank another cup of coffee. The twelve hour shifts never bothered her, but she'd spent the entire weekend staying up late with Caitlin, watching movies and playing games. She'd only been there five days and things hadn't settled down at all. If these missing people weren't found in the next ten hours, Finley would be working overtime, and she was already leaving Caitlin alone while she was on shift. She didn't want her to be alone overnight too. Plus, Finley would more than likely be called in on her standby days because of everyone working overtime, instead of spending the time off with her daughter at the Kennedy Space Center.

It had been two days since Nicole had promised to call back in an a couple hours to discuss the reason behind the impromptu summer visit. Finley could never complain about having Catlin with her for the summer, that was a blessing in itself, even if it was a little hindering at first. Finley was learning to adjust her life to accommodate a teenager in her care, but adding her work schedule into the mix was going to be a challenge.

"Mark, Mark, Mark," Tracey, the Flight Mechanic, radioed into her headset. "Two people in the water, three o'clock."

Finley followed her line of sight.

"They're coming to your six," Finley said, watching them as the helicopter circled around. "Two hundred yards."

"Good eyes, Tracey," Greg, the co-pilot said. "Sector Merritt Island…Search and Rescue 6516. We've located the two passengers, vessel is not in sight. Deploying swimmer. Over," he radioed.

"6516…Sector. Copy," the dispatcher at the base radioed back.

Whenever Finley's aircrew went out for a call, she was dressed for water deployment in a bright orange shorty wetsuit and black booties, as well as a rescue swimmer harness that was hoistable and had an orange manual inflation vest attached with equipment pockets, and a waterproof radio clipped to the shoulder. She wore the same helmet as everyone else inside of the helicopter. When she was preparing to go into the water, she quickly removed the helmet, hanging it by her seat. Then, she pulled on a black dive mask, snorkel, and fins and sat by the open door.

Tracey knelt next to Finley with her hand on

Finley's shoulder. "Target is in sight. Swimmer is ready."

"Roger. We are in a twelve foot hover. The seas are one to two feet. Deploy swimmer," Greg replied. As the pilot, his job was managing the operation and remaining in contact with their base at all times, while handling the helicopter, maintaining a holding pattern, which was the most difficult job on the aircraft, next to the rescue swimmer deploying into the water.

Tracey tapped Finley's shoulder three times to indicate the go ahead order. Finley gave a quick salute and a thumbs up, then she pushed off, free falling the short distance into the water with one hand on her head and the other over her chest in a half-seated position so that her heels entered the water first, then her butt.

"Swimmer is away. Swimmer is in the water," Tracey said

Finley splashed down into the ocean and popped right back up. The salty water tinged her lips as she raised her right arm up over her head with her palm facing forward, indicating she was okay.

"Swimmer is okay," Tracey radioed.

Finley began swimming out of the rotor wash, towards the two people who were bobbing in the water with life vests on.

"Swimmer is at your two o'clock."

"Copy. I've got a visual," Greg replied as he moved the helo up to forty feet above the small waves.

Finley reached the young man and woman easily. "I'm Chief Petty Officer Morris with the United States Coast Guard," she said. Both of the victims were visibly exhausted. "Are either of you injured?"

"No ma'am," the man replied. "Just tired and hungry."

"Where's your boat?" she asked.

"It sank hours ago," the woman answered.

"6516...rescue swimmer. Both survivors are conscious, but fatigued. No apparent injuries. Copy."

"Rescue swimmer...6516, copy. Deploying basket," Greg replied. "Flight Mech, send the basket down to them."

"Roger," Tracey said. "Basket is on the hook." She pushed it out of the open cabin door. Basket is below the cabin door," she added as she began to lower it. "Basket is in the water. Swimmer is at the basket," she finished, watching Finley get the man into the basket. "Survivor is in the basket."

Finley lifted her arm with her hand in the thumbs up position.

"Survivor is ready for pick up."

"Roger. Begin retrieval," Greg said. "Our headwind is starting to pick up," he added.

"Taking the load," Tracey radioed as she began hoisting up the basket.

As soon as the basket was inside the cabin, she helped the man get out. Then, she lowered it back down and waited for Finley to get the woman inside. When she got the signal from Finley, she once again hoisted the basket up and helped the woman out of it.

"Flight Mech, let's get our swimmer and get out of here," Greg said.

"Roger," Tracey replied, sending the hoist hook down.

Finley was waiting for it and quickly attached it to her harness. Then, she threw her arm up with the thumbs up sign.

"Swimmer is on the hook. Swimmer is ready."

"Bring her up," Greg said.

Finley spun around slowly on the cable as she was lifted from the water. When she reached the bottom of the helo, she put her hand out to steady herself. Then, she grabbed the handrail and climbed inside.

"Swimmer is retrieved. Closing cabin door."

Finley put her helmet back on and quickly looked over both people, who seemed to be okay, despite floating in life vests for nearly six hours.

"Alert: eight; Injury: zero," Finley said.

"Sector…Search and Rescue 6516. We are inbound with two survivors. Alert status: eight; Injury status: zero. Copy," Greg said.

"6516…Sector. Copy. EMS is standing by," the dispatcher replied. It was always a precautionary measure to have an ambulance waiting when they were bringing someone in.

*

After they landed and sent the two survivors on their way, the aircrew began the post-flight checklist on the helicopter.

"They were very lucky that the water was warm and the swells were low because of the summer weather," Tracey said.

"Great job, Finley," Greg added as they finished the checklist and headed into the hangar. "Are you meeting us at *Oasis*? We haven't seen you because your schedule changed over the weekend. What's up?"

Finley still hadn't told anyone about her situation. The only thing the Operations Duty officer knew was she had a daughter that came to stay with her. She checked her watch. They had fifteen minutes left in their shift. She was tired from spending most of the day flying around, looking for those two people, and hoped they didn't get called out again before the end of the shift change. "I'm sorry, guys. I had some stuff come up over the weekend. I'm afraid I can't make it tonight either. It's not like I go every week anyway." She shrugged.

Greg walked over to his locker. "Hmm, I still think something's up with you. I'm here if you need to talk."

She knew he meant well, but she wasn't ready to air her dirty laundry through the open cabin door of a helo just yet. "Thanks. I'm fine, really. You guys go have a good time. Hopefully, we don't get called out again."

*

That night, Finley taught Caitlin how to make stuffed bell peppers, a Morris family tradition. They played around in the kitchen together, then enjoyed their crazy creation. Afterwards, they watched the movie SAW III, which scared the hell out of Caitlin, even though she begged Finley to not only let her watch it, but watch it with her. What was she thinking? It was a little gory for Finley, although not really scary. It made her think of the countless nights she'd made Nicole sit up and watch movies that scared the hell out of both of them.

Caitlin was in bed by ten. Finley was finally heading up the stairs to shower and hit her own pillow. She had to be back at the base at six-thirty in the morning and it was already past her bedtime. Halfway to her bedroom she heard her cell phone ringing, which she'd forgotten to carry up with her, so she ran back down the stairs, swiping to answer without even looking at the caller ID. She knew Nicole would call Caitlin's phone if she wanted to talk to her, just as Finley had done for years. It was the reason Finley had bought her the phone in the first place and continued paying the monthly bill for it. She had access to her daughter and vice versa anytime without going through Nicole.

"Hello?" Finley hoped it wasn't the base calling with an emergency. Even when she was on the scheduled shift, if there was a major disaster or an emergency that needed assistance from more than one helo, another aircrew was called in.

"Finley?" Nicole's soft voice was almost a whisper.

"Nic? Why are you whispering?"

"Sorry I didn't call you back. Dave had a bad day and we wound up talking. Anyway, he's asleep now."

Great. She has to sneak around behind her husband's back to call me to discuss our *daughter. What kind of twisted shit is that?* "Well, now that you can talk, I think you have some serious explaining to do."

"I know." Nicole paused. "You have no idea. Caitlin has finally found her attitude and she's been absolutely brutal to live with lately."

"Well, she's a teenager. I hear they are hard to handle. What's so bad that you shipped her off, Nic?" Finley walked out back onto the small deck and stared up at the stars.

"She yells at me and cusses at me. She acts so unhappy all the time. Her grades started slipping last year and she…"

"She what?" Finley was waiting to hear she was having sex or something like that. Hell, the girl hadn't even started her period yet. She was a little bit of a late bloomer, but Finley was sure all of that was about to change and the hormonal imbalance was probably the reason she shot up five inches in a year and the attitude from hell had arrived.

"I'm so mad at her. I don't even know what to say to her. We've been fighting since the day she came home with her schedule for the next school year. She's been constantly arguing with Dave. She refuses to listen to anything he says to her."

"I don't give a shit about Dave. I'll talk to her about respecting adults, but as far as I'm concerned, I don't want to hear his name come out of your mouth. This is about Caitlin. What did she do at school? She didn't quit swimming did she?"

"No. Of course not. I think she's part fish, just like you." Nicole sighed. "She joined that stupid ROTC thing. I went and talked to the principal but he won't let her out of it. Dave even tried talking to him."

Finley cringed when she heard that name again. *ROTC? My little girl has an interest in the military? And she didn't at least talk to me first?* Finley was excited and hurt all at the same time.

"Nic, I'm in the military. If Caitlin wants to see what it's all about, then I'm proud of her. I'm upset that she never expressed the interest to me. I may have stopped her from making a wrong decision, but she is growing up and she can handle it. High School ROTC is a good learning experience for her. She'll either love it or hate it. But don't expect me to be on your side about this. That would be biased considering, don't you think?"

"She doesn't know what that life is like, Finley."

"Well, maybe it's time for her to find out why you left me and tore us apart."

"She's not ready."

"Has she ever asked you about it?"

"Yes," Nicole murmured.

"And what did you say to her? What was the reason you gave our kid for you taking her away from me? Apparently, it wasn't the same bullshit you gave me. Oh, and by the way, how is your dad? I hear he's still kicking."

"That's not funny, Finley. I told her...I told her we would talk about it when she was older."

"She is older! We weren't a whole hell of a lot older than she is when you got pregnant and we got together."

"She's started asking more questions and I can't...Finley. I'm not ready to answer them. And I am damn sure not ready to see her in a uniform. That'll just break my heart."

"Gee, Nic. You sure know how to make a girl feel good. I didn't realize you hated the service that much. But, I'm telling you right now, if she starts asking me questions, I'm going to answer them truthfully." Finally wanted to reach through the phone and smack the woman on the other end.

"I know I can't tell you what to do—"

"You're damn right you can't and your *husband*...," Finley almost choked on the word. "Has no right to tell my daughter anything about the ROTC. It's her choice, and if someone is going to explain the military life to her, it will be me!"

"Why do you always yell at me when we talk?" Nicole's voice was back to a whisper.

Finley knew she was trying to disguise the sadness, but it was still there. She hated hearing it, but Nicole had made her choice. Seeing and hearing how naïve Nicole had gotten over the years made her angry. Something had changed in her. The light that had once shined so brightly when they were younger, was all but gone.

"Well, let's see...we haven't talked for almost seven

years. I had to buy Caitlin a cell phone so that she and I could talk to each other. Plus, you force me to see her through my mother when I come up there. I'm not even going to get started on the other reason. You know why I'm yelling, Nic. Let me just walk out of your life with your child overnight, then send you a wedding invitation for me and my soon to be husband. Then, you tell me if you're not hurt. The years go by, Nic, but the pain is always just below the surface." Finley heard her own voice crack.

"You've changed," Nicole murmured. When Finley didn't say anything, she added, "you sound so bitter."

"Yeah, well you would be too if you were on my end," Finley huffed. "Look, I have to be at the base, and flight ready in six hours. I'll talk to Caitlin about her attitude, but that's it." Finley hung up before Nicole could get another word in.

Damn you, Nicole. Seven fucking years and my heart aches like it was yesterday. Tears stung her eyes as they rolled down her cheeks. Normally, Finley would go for a jog down along the river when she was upset or had Nicole on her mind, but she was reluctant to leave Caitlin asleep upstairs, and she needed to get to bed. Over the past couple of days, Caitlin had become friends with the girl next door, who seemed to be about her age. The girl's mother had offered to keep an eye on Caitlin during the day while Finley was on shift since she was a school teacher and off for the summer, which had worked out perfectly. Caitlin pretty much had free rein of the house, but under the neighbor's supervision. Finley had set down the ground rules, no loud music, no cooking, no boys, no leaving, and no parties. If any of these rules were broken, she'd be going to the base everyday and sitting in the office, staring at four walls while Finley was working. Caitlin showed interest in going to the base, but the smile turned into a frown when she heard about the small room she'd be stuck in for twelve hours a day. Finley promised to take her on a tour of the base in a few weeks, but right now she'd been too busy, and no one knew about her yet. That was a whole different story. One she wasn't ready to share with her friends and colleagues.

Chapter 5

Finley and Caitlin stood in the ticket line outside of NASA's Kennedy Space Center. It was Saturday morning, and the skies were clear. The sun was already beating down over eighty degrees. Crowds of families and a few couples gathered around, waiting to go inside. Little kids were pulling on their mother and father's arms while pointing to the spacecraft statues. Cameras were flashing left and right. Finley saw the smile spread on Caitlin's face when they were finally allowed inside. She grabbed a map and began plotting their course for the day.

After hours of space exhibits and tours, they sat down for lunch in the Astronaut Café where a couple of former astronauts were doing meet and greets, and signing autographs. Caitlin was thrilled to get their signatures and take pictures with them. One lady was nice enough to take a picture of Finley and Caitlin with both of the astronauts.

After lunch, they went on the simulators and took a tour of a mock space shuttle, where Caitlin sat in the Captain's chair, then the pilot's chair as Finley took pictures.

When the park finally closed at five o'clock, Finley and Caitlin were some of the last people to leave. She was happy to see the smile on her daughter's face. She almost didn't want to talk, but the conversation she'd had with Nicole a couple of nights ago was playing on the back of her mind.

"Caitlin, I know something's been bothering you. You know you can talk to me about anything."

"There's nothing to talk about. I had fun today. Thanks for taking me to the space center, Mom."

"You're welcome." Finley looked over at the young girl that looked so much like herself sitting in the passenger seat. She took a deep breath and dove head first. "I talked to your mom. She said you guys have been having problems lately. Do you want to tell me about it?" *Come on, Caitlin. Talk to me.*

"There's nothing going on. Dave and I don't get along, and she thinks I should—"

"Kiss his ass?" Finley finished.

"Yeah, something like that."

"Why aren't you getting along with him?" Finley asked as she checked her mirror and changed lanes on the highway.

"He's not my dad and he never will be. He has no say over what I do. Plus, he treats Mom like shit." She winced for letting the curse word slip. "I'm sorry."

"Where did you learn to swear? I know it wasn't your mother. And you haven't been around me long enough…"

"School, I guess and Dave. He yells and cusses at Mom a lot."

"Oh, really?" Finley didn't like the way this conversation was going. *So she's been standing up for you, Nic, and you're mad at her for that?* "Well, you and I have already had a talk about your swearing. This had better be the last time I hear it. Do you understand me?"

"Yes, ma'am. I'm sorry. I didn't mean to let it slip. I just get so mad at him. You and Mom are my parents. He's nothing to me."

"There's no need to be purposefully mean to him just because your mother and I aren't together anymore, Caitlin. Things happen, and life goes on. You need to be polite. She obviously loves him if she married him." It pained her to say those words, but Caitlin needed to hear them. "Dave is an adult and you will show the utmost respect to adults. Are we clear?"

"Even if he's mean?"

"Unfortunately, yes. If you get frustrated with him and need to talk, you can call me anytime. You know that. I don't want to see you sad. I also don't want you to let him get to you and cause you to be disrespectful."

"She's sad all the time," Caitlin's voice was barely a whisper.

"Who?"

"Mom, she cries a lot. Every time I ask her about it, she tells me that she's fine, but I know she's sad. She forgets I wasn't too little to remember you guys together when we lived with you. Mom was happy and smiled all the time. She's not like that now, and I don't like to see her that way. Plus, he thinks he can tell me what to do at school. You're my mom and my dad all in one. He'll never be anything to me," Caitlin said as tears started to well up in her eyes.

God, this is worse than I thought. "What's going on with school? Why is he sticking his nose in that?"

"I wanted to wait and tell you when I sent you my school pictures, but I guess I can tell you now. I joined the ROTC at school. It's the Air Force ROTC, but I know you were in there too."

Finley smiled and reached over, squeezing her daughter's hand. "You're right. I was in the ROTC at

47

Annandale High. I learned a lot there, and I'm proud of you. I only hope you did this for you and not me, Caitlin. I want you to grow up to be who you are, and do what you want to do. If I had followed my parents' I'd…well I wouldn't be where I am today."

"I know. Grandma talks about you all the time. She tells me how proud of you she is, even if you don't come home much." Caitlin looked at Finley. "I joined because I wanted to. I know swimming takes up a lot of my time, so I don't know if I'll even do it again next year, but right now it's something I wanted to do, so I did it."

"Well, I'm happy for you. Speaking of swimming, how is that going?"

"Great. I've already been told I'll be on the varsity team because the coach was at our division championship meet, scouting me out. He said I might beat your record while I'm at Annandale," she beamed cheerfully.

"Oh, really? You think you can out swim me, kiddo?" Finley laughed.

"I don't know, but I'm going to try." Caitlin smiled.

"How would you like to see what I really do every day?" Finley asked.

"Really? I can come to work with you?" Finley heard that excited little girl that she missed so much.

"Sure. I'll talk to my Operations Duty Officer and see if I can get you up in a bird for a training mission or something."

"Wow! I can't wait. Mom was so mad when I told her about ROTC. She even tried to get me out of it, but I guess she couldn't. Dave yelled at me, and then he called the principal or something. I wanted to call you so badly."

"Well, I think you're old enough to make a decision like that. You're curious about the military and there is nothing wrong with that, obviously." She grinned. "I'm sorry your mom gave you a hard time about it. She doesn't like the military, and Dave, well I'm not going there." She'd definitely be making a trip to Charleston to have a face-to-face talk with that son-of-a-bitch. "Hey, how about some ice cream?" Finley asked as she turned into the Dairy Queen on their highway exit.

*

Friday morning, Finley's next shift day, she walked into the office of the Operations Duty Officer. He was the assistant to the commanding officer of the air base and the one who handled the aircrew shifts, flight schedules, call outs, and so on. She talked with him often.

"How's it going, Morris?" CDR. Douglas asked, sipping a cup of coffee.

"Good. I took my kid out to Kennedy yesterday."

"Oh, my daughter and son loved it there. They both wanted to be astronauts when we left," he laughed. "Did she have a good time?"

"Yeah, but she doesn't want to be an astronaut." Finley grinned. "She joined the ROTC at school, which was news to me."

He nodded. "Does she want to be a Coastie?"

"I don't know. She's also an award-winning swimmer like I was."

"I'll talk to Captain Shultz and see if we can get her up in a helo, so she can see what you do every day."

Finley smiled. "That would definitely trump the space center."

"It does for me too," he said.

Finley walked out of his office and headed over to

her locker to get her gear bag and do her preflight checklist. She didn't bother to tell anyone else about Caitlin because she wasn't prepared for all of the questions she'd be faced with.

*

Later that afternoon, Finley was part of a routine training mission when a call came in for a distressed boat thirty miles away. The helicopter turned around and plotted a course towards the sinking sailboat. The forty foot sloop had begun taking on water and was just about completely submerged by the time the helo spotted it.

"Sector Merritt Island…Search and Rescue 6516. We are on scene. The vessel is 75% submerged. Two survivors still onboard. Deploying swimmer. Over."

"6516…Sector. Copy."

"Looks like neither is wearing a life vest," Tracey said.

Finley took a peek out at the boat when she sat on the edge of the open cabin door. The boat was on its port side, so the mast was down in the water and wouldn't be a hindrance as she was lowered. She quickly attached the hoist clip to her swimmer harness and gave Tracey a thumbs up.

"Swimmer is ready."

"Roger. Begin hoist," Greg replied.

Tracey tapped Finley on the chest once to indicate they had the go ahead. Then, she moved behind her and tapped her shoulder to signal she was starting the maneuver. "Taking the load," she said into her radio as the hoist lifted Finley a few inches off the floor of the helo.

Finley adjusted her harness and gave another

thumbs up.

"Swimmer is outside of the cabin. Swimmer is being lowered."

Finley kept her hands on the V of her harness as she moved closer and closer to the water. The helicopter was in a hover forty foot above sea level and forty yards from the sinking vessel to keep them out of the rotor wash.

"Swimmer is in the water. Swimmer is away," Tracey said as Finley raised her arm up with an open palm. She watched her release the clasp for the hoist and begin swimming towards the boat.

"I'm Chief Petty Officer Morris with the Coast Guard," Finley said, treading water a few feet away from the vessel. She noticed a man further up and a woman halfway in the water, clinging to the side of the craft. "I'm going to get you out of here, but you have to come off of the boat to do that."

"I'm going to drown!" the woman screamed.

"Calm down, ma'am. Everything will be fine. What's your name?"

"Barbara," she yelled. "I can't swim! I'm going to die!"

Finley turned around and gave the signal for the basket to be lowered. Then, she swam a little closer when a small wave pushed her up. "Okay, Barbara. You have to let go of the boat. I've got you," she said, putting her hands on the woman's waist.

When the woman felt the touch, she let go of the boat and spun to cling to Finley's head in one swift motion. Finley took a deep breath before she was shoved under the water. She made a quick adjustment that broke the woman's hold on her. Then, she rose to the surface and pulled the woman to her from behind. "Be still and let me do the work," she said as she began swimming backwards towards the basket.

"Swimmer is approaching the basket with survivor one," Tracey radioed, waiting for the signal from Finley to hoist the woman up.

The woman began to panic when they swam into the rotor wash. The noise from the helo was loud, so she couldn't hear Finley talking to her.

"Barbara, you have to get inside the basket!" Finley yelled, holding it steady with one hand, while keeping the woman from going under with the other.

The woman finally grabbed a hold of the basket and Finley shoved her up inside of it. "Hold on to the inside handles right here," she added before giving the thumbs up signal.

"Survivor is ready," Tracey said.

"Roger. Begin hoist," Greg replied.

Finley swam to the side as the basket slowly began to rise out of the water.

"Swimmer is away."

"6516...rescue swimmer. Be advised, survivor one is distressed. No visible injuries. Over."

"Rescue swimmer...6516. Copy," Greg said.

Tracey pulled the basket inside the helo. Then, she helped the panic-stricken woman out of it and into a jump seat, before handing her a dry towel.

Finley made it back to the boat quickly, where the man was still clinging to the handrail on the top of the cabin near the mast. "Sir, I need you to come off the boat and into the water," she said.

"No. I'm not leaving my boat," he yelled.

Finley shook her head. "Your boat is sinking and in another few minutes, it'll be at the bottom of the Atlantic.

Barbara is waiting for you in the helo. I need you to get into the water."

"No!" he shouted. I'm not going anywhere!"

The man was acting delusional and she had no other choice, but to get on the boat with him. "Sir, I can't let you drown. You have to come with me," she growled, spinning him around. He was bleeding from a large gash on the left side of his head near his hairline and the entire left side of his face was covered in blood. "That explains it," she murmured, realizing his head injury was probably making him delirious.

"6516...rescue swimmer. Be advised, survivor two has a stage one head injury. Over," she radioed.

"Rescue swimmer...6516. Copy."

She quickly gave the signal for the basket, then yanked him free of the rail he was holding. Finley dove into the water behind him, pulling him to the surface as he flailed around. "I've got you. Be still and I'll have you out of the water in a minute," she yelled over the loud noise of the helo.

"Basket is in the water," Tracey said as she watched Finley push the man inside of it. Then, she squeezed herself in with him, holding his head up. "Survivor and swimmer are in the basket," she radioed. "He must have lost consciousness," she added as it began to ascend towards her. "Basket is at the cabin door," she said, pulling it inside. "Basket is inside. Cabin door is closed."

"Roger," Greg said.

Finley got out of the basket, then she helped Tracey get the man onto the backboard that she'd laid on the floor, all while kneeling in the tight space. He was breathing, but was unconscious and his pulse was low.

"He's lost a lot of blood," Finley said when she put

her helmet on. "Survivor one, Alert: nine; Injury: zero. Survivor two, Alert: zero; Injury: seven," she added, giving the pilot her assessment.

"Sector...Search and Rescue 6516. Be advised we are inbound with two. Survivor one, Alert: nine; Injury: zero. Survivor two, Alert: zero; Injury: seven. Survivor two is bleeding from a head wound and is unconscious. Over," he radioed.

"6516...Sector. Copy. Reroute to Cocoa Beach Memorial. Over," dispatch radioed back, telling them to head directly to the nearest hospital.

"Sector...6516. Copy on the reroute."

Finley put a large bandage on the man's head, and applied pressure to try and stop the bleeding as she glanced at the woman in the jump seat next to her. She was obviously still terrified. Her skin was pale white, her eyes were closed, and she had a death grip on the shoulder strap of the seatbelt. Finley wished she could reassure her that everything would be all right, and they'd be on the ground soon, but the noise inside the helo was extremely loud. There was no use in talking to anyone who didn't have a headset on. She relied on hand signals to communicate with the survivors who were alert.

"Cocoa Beach Memorial...Search and Rescue 6516. Be advised, we are two minutes out. Over," Greg radioed to the hospital.

"Rescue 6516...Cocoa Beach. Copy. Emergency team is standing by."

Finley reached over, tapping the woman's knee. She jerked back, opening her eyes widely. Finely held her hand up to calm her. Then, she held up two fingers and tapped the top of her wristwatch to indicate two more minutes.

"Crew report, ready for approach?" Greg asked.

"Ready," Tracey replied.

Finley checked the man one last time. "Ready," she said.

Thirty seconds later, the helo began to descend in slow motion until they felt the slight bump of the ground. Greg powered the helo down to an idle and Tracey slid the cabin door open. Finley jumped out, pulling the head of the backboard out with her. A handful of doctors and nurses ran across the helicopter pad, pushing a gurney. Finley helped them slid the man off the board and onto the stretcher as she gave a brief update on his condition. Then, as they were rushing him into the hospital, Tracey helped the woman out of the helo, and another nurse was waiting to walk her inside.

"Sector Merritt Island...Search and Rescue 6516. Be advised, we are airborne. Over," Greg radioed as they took off from the hospital. "Finley, are you good to continue 010?" he asked, checking to see if she had enough energy to go back to their training mission.

"Roger on 010," she answered.

Sector Merritt Island...Search and Rescue 6516. Permission to continue Training Mission 010. Over," Greg radioed.

"6516...Sector. Negative on TM010. Return to base," the dispatcher replied.

"Sector...6516. Copy. Be advised, we are fifty minutes from bingo fuel. Over," Greg radioed, letting the operations officer know they have enough fuel to continue the training mission.

"Search and Rescue 6516...Sector ODO. Roger on the bingo mark. Double time back to base. Over," CDR. Douglas, the Operations Duty Officer replied, taking over the dispatch radio.

"6516…Sector. Roger on the double time," Greg said. He wasn't sure what was wrong, but he knew something was up. He and the co-pilot were the only two who could hear the dispatch radio calls. Everyone else in the aircrew was on a different channel. He pushed the button for the aircrew channel and said, "We've been pushed up to double time and rerouted back to base."

"What's going on?" Finley asked.

"No idea," he replied.

When they touched down, Greg powered down the helo and everyone climbed out. The loud speaker in the hangar announced, "Chief Morris, you have an urgent message in the Command Master Chief's office."

The color in Finley's face drained as she ran to the nearest phone in the hangar.

"This is AST Chief Petty Officer Morris."

"Chief, your neighbor called thirty minutes ago. They were in a car accident, but everyone is okay. She said to tell you Caitlin was fine, just a little shook up, and they are back at home."

"Okay, thank you for letting me know." Finley hung up the phone and turned around to face the Operations Duty Officer, who had come out of the dispatch office when the helo had arrived.

"Is everything okay?" he asked.

"My daughter's been spending time with my neighbor and they were in a car accident."

"Oh, no. Are they all right?"

"Yes, sir. Everyone's fine. My daughter is a little shook up though."

"You're relieved for the rest of the day. I'm looking forward to meeting this young lady, if she's up for flying tomorrow. Capt. Schultz gave the go ahead for your request to bring her on a training mission."

"Thank you. She'll probably be too excited to sleep." Finley smiled, before rushing to change out of her shorty wetsuit and back into her flight suit. She didn't notice her two friends watching her like she was a stranger to them, after overhearing the conversation.

*

Caitlin ran out of the house, diving into Finley's arms as soon as she'd stepped out of the SUV. Finley picked her up off the ground slightly before setting her back down. Tears streamed down Caitlin's face, and Finley felt a few of her own mix with them on her cheek.

"Mom, I was so scared."

"I know, baby girl." Finley wiped the tears from Caitlin's face and walked inside the neighbor's house with her.

Finley found out the accident had been the other drivers' fault. Her neighbor and her neighbor's daughter had a few cuts and scratches from the broken glass, and some bruising from the airbags since they had been sitting up front. Caitlin didn't have a scratch on her thanks to her seat belt and the fact that she was in the back seat.

As soon as they walked back over to Finley's house, she turned to Caitlin. "You'd better let me call your mom. She's liable to freak out."

"I know," Caitlin said.

"I have some good news," Finley added.

Caitlin raised an eyebrow, waiting in suspense as she plopped down on the couch.

"You're coming to work with me tomorrow and flying with us on a training mission...if you want to of course. I won't twist your arm or anything." Finley grinned.

"Oh, my God! Yes!" Caitlin cheered.

"That is, unless you're too sore. I'm sure you'll feel stiff in the morning. I've been in a couple of fender benders over the years, and the next day is always hell."

"I still want to go. I'll be fine."

"Okay." Finley smiled and headed up stairs to make the phone call she dreaded. She decided to place another call first.

"Mom?" she murmured when the line picked up.

"Hey, Finley!" Her mother's voice sounded happy. "How are things going with Caitlin there?"

"Great. I love having her around. I miss her so much."

"I'm glad you're spending time with her. That kid needs you in her life more than you know."

"I know, Mom," she sighed.

"You sound like something's bothering you. What is it? Are you being transferred again?"

"No. Not for another few months at least," Finley replied. *That's the least of my worries at the moment,* she thought. "Caitlin's been hanging out next door with my neighbor's daughter while I'm on shift. They're the same age and the mother is a teacher, so she's off for the summer. Anyway they were all in a car accident earlier today—"

"Oh, my God!"

"She's fine, Mom. They're all okay. She's just a little shook up. I think it scared her pretty good."

"Thank God she's all right." Jackie Morris paused as if a light bulb went off. "Ah, I see why you're calling. You haven't told Nicole."

Finley sighed. "Uh huh."

"Unfortunately, accidents happen, honey. The good

thing is, Caitlin wasn't injured. Nicole will understand. There is no better place for that child to be than with you, especially right now."

"Thanks, Mom."

"I love you both," her mother said.

"Love you too."

She hung up the phone and finished changing clothes. She even contemplated having a drink first. It was already difficult telling her mother, even though Caitlin was fine. Surprisingly, she took it well. Nicole would be upset, and Finley wasn't going to be the one holding her to reassure her their daughter was okay. That thought gutted her. Needing some renewed energy, Finley stripped off her flight suit and jumped in the hot shower to wash away the stickiness of the saltwater and revitalize her brain.

*

Finley toweled off and pulled on a pair of dark blue shorts and a light gray shirt with USCG on the front of it. Then, she sat on the edge of her bed and scrolled through the contact list in her phone.

"Finley?" Nicole questioned, answering the call on the second ring.

"Hey. Caitlin's fine, but I wanted to tell you she was involved in a small accident this afternoon."

"What!" Nicole's voice changed drastically. "What do you mean accident? Where is she? What happened?"

"Calm down, she's okay. She was with my neighbor and her daughter, and they were in an accident. Everyone is fine."

"Oh my God, no!" Finley could hear Nicole begin to cry.

"Listen to me, Nic. Our baby girl is fine. There isn't a scratch on her. It scared her more than anything."

"How could you let this happen?" Nicole cried.

"I didn't *let* anything happen. It was an accident. She could have easily been in the car with me or you. The point is…she didn't get hurt. No one did, actually."

"Where is she? Are you sure she's okay?" Nicole sniffled.

"Yes. I promise. She's downstairs on the couch, but you need to get it together before you talk to her."

"I'm fine. Please let me talk to her, Finley."

"Okay. Hold on." Finley walked down the stairs. "Here, it's your mother," she said, handing Caitlin the phone. Then, she went into the kitchen to pour herself a drink.

As soon as Caitlin hung up the phone, Finley joined her on the couch. "Everything okay?"

"Yeah. Mom's a little upset, but I told her I was all right. We talked about Uncle Mike's car accident. She said that's why she was so upset."

Finley nodded. "We love you so much, Caitlin. We don't want to lose you like we lost him." Finley wrapped her arm around Caitlin's shoulders and kissed the side of her head. "You seem okay, so I think you're flight ready."

"Really!" Caitlin's eyes lit up.

"Why not." Finley smiled.

"Yes! Thanks, Mom. You're the greatest!" Caitlin wrapped her arms around Finley and squeezed. "By the way, what took so long? Marilyn went nuts when you didn't answer your cell. I had to call the base for her."

"I left the operations office phone number for her. Anyway, I was in the air on a training mission, then out on a call. After someone talked to her, they diverted us back to the base. That's when I got the message."

"Oh, what was the call for?"

"A sinking sailboat with two people on it."

"Cool." Caitlin smiled.

Chapter 6

Finley pulled through the gates of the air station and parked her SUV in the usual spot. Caitlin was sitting next to her dressed in jeans, one of Finley's USCG t-shirts, and sneakers.

"Come on, kiddo." Finley stepped out of the truck and put her baseball cap on as she walked towards the main hangar. Caitlin fell instep beside her.

CDR. Douglas walked out of his office, dressed in the dark blue BDU pants and matching button shirt of his daily work uniform. He had a matching baseball cap on with his rank insignia in the center. He looked from Finley to Caitlin and back again.

"She looks just like you, Morris."

"Thank you, sir." Finley smiled. "This is my daughter, Caitlin Morris. Caitlin, this is Commander Douglas. He's the Senior Operations Duty Officer for USCG Air Station Merritt Island. He oversees all of Search and Rescue."

"It's nice to meet you, sir," Caitlin said.

"Likewise." He smiled. "How old are you?"

"Thirteen, sir," she answered.

"Welcome to Air Station Merritt Island," he said, holding his hand out. Caitlin quickly shook it. "Your mother is one of the best Helicopter Rescue Swimmers I've ever seen. She's well respected around here. I'd trust her with my own life."

"Thank you, sir," Finley said.

"She's going to need a flight suit and full gear to go up in the helo. I have your aircrew scheduled for Training Mission 025 this morning."

"Great. I'll get her suited up."

"Morris," he said, pulling Finley aside. "If you guys get a call while you're out there, you'll have to take her with you as if she were a training cadet. I've already briefed your crew."

"I understand," Finley replied. "I'll go over everything with her."

As soon as they walked out of the operations office, Tracy and Greg appeared. Finley felt bad for not telling them, but then again she hadn't told them much about her personal life.

"Caitlin, this is Lieutenant Gregory Ballard. He's a helicopter pilot. And this is AMT Petty Officer Second Class Tracy Pollack. She's a Flight Mechanic. Guys, this is my daughter, Caitlin Morris."

"Hi," Tracy and Greg said together.

"It's nice to meet you both." Caitlin smiled and walked closer to the large orange and white helicopter parked nearby.

"God, Fin, she looks just like you," Tracy said.

"Yeah, she's a great kid."

"This is a surprise. I had no idea you had kids. How old is she?" Greg said.

"She's the only one, and she's thirteen. I'm sorry I didn't tell you guys. I don't talk much about my life, or that side of it anyway. Caitlin lives with her other mother in South Carolina."

"Wow," Tracey murmured.

"She was having some problems at home, so she came to spend the remainder of the summer with me. It happened out of the blue. She's been here about a week."

"That must suck. I don't know if I could live that far away from my child," Tracy said.

Finley turned her head to look at Caitlin. Greg had walked over to tell her all about the helo, something that would take days if anyone gave him enough time. He also gave her an old flight suit and searched around until they found a pair of boots that would fit her. Caitlin loved every minute of it.

"I was kind of forced to let her go when her mother left me and took Caitlin with her."

"Aw, Finley. I'm sorry."

"It's okay. It was a long time ago, and we've all learned to deal with it, I guess."

Tracy watched Greg with Caitlin. "It looks like he's recruiting her," she laughed.

"She just joined the ROTC at her school."

"Really?"

"Yeah." Finley smiled. "Pissed her mom off pretty good."

Tracy laughed. "Is she a swimmer?"

"Yes. She's won some awards. Now that she's about to start at my old high school, she's going after my records," Finley chuckled.

"Do you think she'll beat them?"

"I hope she does." Finley smiled.

*

After going over the helicopter safety instructions, Finley outfitted Caitlin with a helmet and an aircrew survival vest, similar to the one Rescue Swimmer's wear with the integrated harness attached, except the aircrew vest is black and the swimmer vest is orange. Then, she changed from her own flight suit to the orange, shorty wetsuit for deployment. After that, she stuffed her mask, fins, and snorkel into her flight bag, and pulled on her survival vest and harness. She checked the radio on her vest to make sure it was fully charged, then grabbed her helmet and headed out to the helo.

"Today's training mission involves swimmer deployment. We'll do a couple of hoists down and back up. If the seas stay calm, we'll move in so Finley can jump out and hoist back up," Greg stated.

"Roger," Tracy acknowledged.

"Caitlin, your job for today is to stay in your jump seat with your seatbelt on. You'll be able to hear us talking on the radio in your helmet. If you need to say anything, make sure you speak loud and clearly so we can understand you. It'll be noisy up there. If there is a lot of turbulence, it can get bumpy as well."

"Yes, sir," Caitlin replied.

"Lock and load," Greg said.

He and the co-pilot, LTJG. Dan Kloss, walked to the front doors of the helo, while Tracy opened the cabin door. Finley climbed in first, showing Caitlin where to sit. She helped her get strapped in and put her helmet on. Then, she and Tracy took their seats and pulled their helmets on.

Greg flipped the switches and started the twin turbine engines.

"Closing cabin door," Tracey said.

"Roger," Greg replied, still going through his pre-flight list as the engines warmed up. "Crew report. Ready for departure?" he asked.

"Roger," Tracy and Finley both said.

"Sector Merritt Island…Search and Rescue 6516. We are ready for departure. Over."

"6516…Sector. You are cleared for takeoff," the dispatcher replied.

Finley glanced over at Caitlin who had one eye on the pilots and the other on the window. A huge smile spread across her face as they rose off the ground, causing Finley to grin as well. There was nothing like going up in a helo. No matter how many times she'd done it, she still got the same ball of nerves and excitement in her gut. When they were headed out for a call, that ball of nerves was doused with adrenaline.

The land around them quickly disappeared as they headed out over the Atlantic Ocean. They made a few passes over some fishing boats, then continued further out.

"How are you doing?" Finley asked, looking at Caitlin.

"Great!" she beamed.

Tracy laughed. "She's a natural."

"Must take after her mom," Greg added, giving her a thumbs up.

It took another ten minutes for them to reach the designated coordinates for their training mission.

"Sector…Search and Rescue 6516. We are on the mark. Commencing with TM025. Over," Greg radioed.

"6516…Sector. Copy."

"Here we go," he radioed to the crew.

"You stay there unless Greg or Tracy tell you otherwise," Finley said, grabbing Caitlin's shoulder.

"Yes, ma'am."

"The seas are one to two feet. I'm going to take us down to a ten foot ceiling. Finley, are you good to jump?"

"Roger," she replied.

"Opening cabin door," Tracy said.

Finley buckled the gunner belt around her waist for safety as she sat down and swung her legs outside of the helo.

"Ten foot ceiling and holding," Greg announced.

Tracey tapped Finley on the chest and Finley gave her a thumbs up.

"Swimmer is ready."

"Sector...6516. Deploying swimmer for TM025. Over."

"6516...Sector. Copy."

"Deploy swimmer," Greg said.

Tracey tapped Finley on the shoulder three times.

Finley released the gunner belt and pushed off. She held one arm over her chest and the other over her head as she prepared to hit the water.

"Swimmer is in the water," Tracey said. When Finley threw her arm up with her palm facing out, Tracey added, "Swimmer is okay."

Finley swam out of the rotor wash as the helo rose up to fifty foot above her head. Then, treaded water as they went through the maneuver to hoist her back up.

Tracey walked over to Caitlin and unbuckled her seat belt. Then, she clasped a gunner's tether to her harness and brought her to the edge of the open door.

"Wow!" Caitlin exclaimed as she peered down at her mother, bobbing in the sea below.

"Be careful," Finley radioed, waving up at her.

Tracey helped Caitlin back to her seat, then went to work hoisting Finley back up. They went through the same drill two more times, then began lowering her on the hoist and bringing her back up.

Finley had gone in the water and been retrieved half a dozen times when Greg's radioed crackled to life.

"Search and Rescue 6516...Sector Merritt Island. A missing diver has been reported fifteen miles east of Melbourne Beach. Divert to the area and commence aerial search. Over," the dispatcher said.

"Sector...6516. Copy on the diversion. Be advised, we are fifteen minutes out. Departing for Melbourne Beach. Over."

Tracey closed the cabin door and the helicopter headed towards the missing diver.

"Sector...6516. How long has the diver been down? Over."

"6516...Sector. We are unsure at this time. She had a two hour tank with thirty minutes reserve and has not been seen since she went in three hours ago. Over."

"Sector...6516. Copy."

"We have no idea what to expect if we find her," Greg radioed the crew.

"She could be bent," Finley added, referring to diver decompression sickness.

"True," Greg replied. "Sector...6516. How far is the nearest recompression chamber, in case the survivor is bent? Over."

"6516...Sector. Melbourne Medical Center, approximately thirty minutes from the last known location. Over."

"Sector...6516. Copy. Be advised, we are ten minutes out. Over."

"6516...Sector. Copy."

As soon as they were within five minutes of the last known location, Tracey opened the cabin door. She and Finley strapped on gunner belts that tethered them to the helo in case they fell out as they leaned over, peering down at the water. More than likely, the diver was wearing a black diving suit, which would prove extremely difficult to find in the dark blue mass of the Atlantic Ocean.

They passed over the dive boat that had sent the mayday call and kept going, following the current further out to sea. The waves were one to two feet and a small headwind was blowing at eight to ten knots. Essentially, the conditions were quite calm and ideal for diving.

"Do you want to drop a drift buoy?" Tracey asked. They usually put a buoy in the water to see the rate and direction of the current when they were looking for someone who had fallen off a boat, but sometimes they also used it to help locate missing divers.

"No," Greg replied. "I'm going to take us to a thirty foot ceiling and start passing over a grid in the direction the current is flowing. If she hasn't surfaced by now, she got hung up on a wreck or something. If she has come up, she probably drifted pretty far."

Finley pushed her helmet shield up and began scanning the water with a pair of binoculars. Tracey did the same thing.

"6516…Sector. The boaters radioed that the woman is wearing a dark, shorty wetsuit, but has a hot pink tank with her gear. Over."

"Sector…6516. Copy. Guys, we're looking for a bright pink scuba tank."

"Mark, Mark, Mark!" Finley yelled. "She's at your four o'clock, Greg!" she added, tossing the binoculars to the side as she grabbed her mask, snorkel, and fins, preparing to go in the water.

Greg quickly spun the helo around to vector into position. He noticed the woman was floating in an odd position.

"Sector...6516. Diver located. Deploying swimmer. Over."

"6516...Sector. Copy," the dispatcher replied.

"Swimmer is ready," Tracey said.

"She doesn't look good. I'm going to take us down to twelve feet so you can jump. I want to keep her out of the rotor wash," Greg said to Finley, who gave Tracey a thumbs up. "Twelve and holding. Deploy swimmer," he added.

Tracey tapped Finley on the shoulder three times to signal she had the go ahead. Caitlin watched as her mother quickly pushed off from her sitting position at the cabin door and disappeared.

The salty water was warm when Finley splashed down. She quickly held her arm up, indicating that she was fine. Then, she swam towards the diver as fast as she could.

"Swimmer is in the water. Swimmer is okay and away," Tracey said.

Greg put the helo in an autopilot holding pattern while he waited.

The woman was on her side with her head barely out of the water. She was floating because the auto-inflatable vest she was wearing had inflated.

"Ma'am, can you hear me? I'm Chief petty Officer Morris with the Coast Guard."

The woman's eyes fluttered open. "My whole body hurts," she murmured. "It's so bad," she cried.

"I'm going to help you," Finley said, grabbing her from behind and removing the dive equipment, letting it fall to the ocean floor. "Are you having any difficulty breathing?"

"No," the woman said. "I have a massive headache

and all of my bones hurt like they're broken."

"6516…rescue swimmer. Be advised, survivor is bent. Over."

"Swimmer…6516. Copy."

Finley signaled for the sling and began swimming the diver towards the helo's rotor wash as Tracey lowered the hoist. When they reached it, Finley put the sling around the woman, securing it tightly. Then, she connected it to her harness.

"Okay, we're about to get picked up. I'm going to hold onto you from behind. We're both attached to the cable, so it is going to lift us together. Are you ready?" Finley asked.

"Yes," the woman murmured, barely opening her eyes.

Finley gave the thumbs up signal and Tracey started the hoist. When the cable started to spin, Finley spread her fins out wide to counter balance and stall the spin. Once they were inside, Tracey helped Finley get the woman strapped into the litter to keep her from getting tossed about in the helo. Then, Finley quickly put the oxygen mask over her nose and mouth and started an IV line to give her fluids in case of dehydration.

"Alert: three; Injury: seven," Finley radioed, giving Greg the status report.

"Sector…6516. Survivor has been retrieved. Alert: three; Injury: seven. She is bent. Repeat: survivor is bent. Diverting to Melbourne Medical Center. Over."

"6516…Sector. Copy."

Greg flew them at near maximum speed. Finley checked the woman's vitals, then she gave her daughter a quick pat on the knee before strapping into her jump seat. Caitlin gave her a thin smile, then trained her eyes back on the woman lying in front of her.

"Melbourne Medical...Search and Rescue 6516. We are inbound with a bent diver. ETA: three minutes. Over."

"Rescue 6516...Melbourne Medical. Copy. Standing by."

"Crew report. Ready for approach?" Greg asked.

"Ready," Tracey and Finley said.

"Wheels down," Greg announced.

Tracey slid the cabin door open and Finley jumped out, pulling the head of the litter out with her. Tracey climbed out, grabbing the foot of it as hospital personnel raced towards them with a gurney. They worked together, moving the woman off the litter and onto the stretcher. Finley updated them on the woman's condition while Tracey climbed back into the helo to store the litter.

When Finley got back inside, Greg asked, "How bad was it?"

"She was in bad shape. She probably saw she was low on oxygen and inflated that vest when she was down pretty deep. It shot her to the surface quickly," Finley replied, shaking her head.

"Is she going to live?" Caitlin asked.

"Oh, yeah." Finley smiled. "She'll have to be in a hyperbaric chamber for about four or five hours, but she'll be fine. I don't think she was sick enough to suffer any long-term effects."

Caitlin nodded and turned her head to watch the pilots as Tracey closed the cabin door.

"Ready for takeoff," Tracey said as she strapped into her jump seat.

"Sector Merritt Island...Search and Rescue 6516. We are airborne and five minutes out from bingo fuel. Over," he radioed as they lifted off.

"6516...Sector. Copy. Return to base," the dispatcher answered.

"Mom, what is bingo fuel?" Caitlin asked.

"Bingo is just enough fuel to get you back to base. So, it's kind of like when the fuel light comes on in the car, and you have about thirty miles of reserve fuel to get to a gas station."

"Are we out of gas?" Caitlin squeaked.

"No," Finley laughed. "We'll be fine."

"Ok." Caitlin nodded.

*

When they landed, Caitlin walked around with aircrew as they did their post flight check. Then, the maintenance crew began the refueling procedures while they went to debrief in the operations office.

"You had yourself a heck of a day, kid," CDR. Douglas said to Caitlin. "Got to see all kinds of action."

"Yes, sir. Thank you for letting me come here today and fly with my mom."

"You're welcome," he replied, shaking her hand. "Easiest recruiting that I've ever done," he said to Finley.

"I'm not sure about that," Finley laughed. "She was pretty wide-eyed between the ghastly woman in the litter and bingo fuel."

"First time jitters. We all get them." He shrugged.

Finley smiled as they walked out of his office.

"It was fun showing you what we do," Tracey said. "Your mom needs to bring you around more often, and I don't mean just the base," she added, looking at Finley.

"She's only here for a couple more weeks."

"Great. Let's do a barbecue or something," Tracey

replied.

"The Fourth of July is next week," Greg commented, walking up on the conversation.

"Can we have a party, Mom?" Caitlin asked. "And get fireworks?"

"Actually, you can see the city fireworks show in the river really good from her house," Tracey declared.

"Cool," Caitlin said. "Can we, Mom? Please?" she asked with a big smile on her face.

"We'll be on standby, guys," Finley stated.

"So, we won't drink. No big deal," Greg retorted. "Come on, Fin…" he begged like a little kid. "You have the best place for it, right down the road from the river."

Finley rolled her eyes. "Oh, all right," she huffed.

Tracy winked at Caitlin. "We're still on for tomorrow, right?" she said to Finley.

"Yes." Finley nodded.

"Sounds good." Tracey smiled as she turned to go finish her flight maintenance log for the shift.

"Come on, you can hang out with me while I do my paperwork. Then, we'll shift change and be out of here," Finley said to Caitlin.

*

After dinner, Caitlin called Nicole to tell her about her day, which only added fuel to the fire. Finley didn't feel like hearing Nicole's multiple reasons for why she shouldn't have taken her to the base, up in a helicopter, or out on a search and rescue mission. Instead, she poured herself a tumbler glass of bourbon, which was filled with ice, and walked the two blocks down to the river to clear her head. She had only taken a few sips from the glass when she heard a voice.

"You miss her don't you?"

Finley turned her head as Caitlin sat down next to her. "What makes you say that?" she asked.

"She does the same thing when something's on her mind. We don't live by the water, but she goes out back and sits in the swing, usually with a drink in her hand too. I think this is when she's thinking about you."

"How'd you get to be so smart?" Finley grinned at her.

"I take after you." Caitlin smiled.

"Yeah, you do. More than I ever realized." Finley sipped the last of the whiskey and swirled the empty glass of ice around. "I'm glad you're here with me. I've missed you a lot."

"I've missed you too, Mom. I don't blame you. You know."

"Blame me? For what?"

"Us leaving. I don't blame you for it."

"Thanks, kiddo." Finley put her arm around Caitlin. "What's the story your mom told you?"

"Probably not the real one." Caitlin stared out at the lapping water. "She said things just weren't working out, and you were too busy for a family."

Finley felt a tear run down her cheek. She sighed, thankful it was dark out so Caitlin couldn't see the sadness in her eyes. "Your Grandma Wetherby and I don't get along, which you know. She helped your mom believe that the military life wasn't what she wanted or you needed, on top of other things. So, she moved away and took you with her. I guess Dave came into the picture a couple of years later."

"Mom only married Dave because of grandma.

She's not happy with him. I don't even think they do it."

"Caitlin!" Finley raised her eyebrows. "You should not be talking like that young lady."

"Sorry."

"Besides, I don't want to even think about your mother and him." Finley shivered at the thought.

"I know I always see you at Grammy's house when you visit, but when was the last time you saw Mom in person?"

Finley held her breath and pictured the last time she saw her.

"Don't do this, Nic. I love you, and I love that baby more than anything in this world."

"I have to go, Finley. This is better for all of us. I'll always love you, and she'll always be our *daughter."*

That was seven years ago, and the last time Finley had seen Nicole Wetherby face to face.

"The day she left with you. I called her a few times and tried to see her once, but after that, she made me keep all contact through your Grammy. I couldn't bear seeing her anyway."

"I hate her for breaking our family up," Caitlin cried.

"Never say you hate your mother, Caitlin. I don't ever want to hear that again. I know you're upset with her, and that's fine, but you don't hate her. Please don't think I hate her either. I could never hate her. She gave me you, and the best years of my life. I'll always love her. I don't agree with her choices, and I know she had a lot of help with those choices back then, but life goes on."

"I want to stay here with you, Mom."

"You mean after the summer?"

"Yeah."

Finley's heart broke. She wondered just how bad things were in Nicole's house. She wished with everything she had that she could move Caitlin in with her permanently, but it was impossible. "You have school waiting for you in a few weeks and your mom misses you."

"Well, I miss you, and I never get to see you. You don't yell at me, and you don't have some jerk bossing you around. We have fun together. I like it here with you, Mom."

"I know, kiddo," Finley whispered, hugging Caitlin. *I know.* Her chest felt constricted. She was still on the edge of a sharp sword, trying to decide whether or not she wanted to spend the next three years as an instructor at the swimmer school. Knowing how difficult life at home was for Caitlin, it would be twice as bad for her. She didn't think she could stand to live in the same city as Nicole and her husband. She'd never felt so torn.

"Hey, Mom…" Caitlin said as they began walking back to the house. "What's up with you and Tracey?"

"Tracey? What do you mean?"

"Are you dating?" Caitlin asked. "You can tell me if you are."

"What? No," Finley laughed. "What gave you that idea?"

"You seem pretty close. She likes you. I can tell."

Finley smiled and shook her head. "I promise, she and I are not into each other."

"Then what are you doing with her tomorrow?"

"She goes on runs with me sometimes. It's not a date, if that's what you thought."

"Is she a lesbian, too?"

"Yes."

"So, why not date her?"

77

"You sure are full of questions all of a sudden."

Caitlin shrugged.

Finley thought about the last woman she'd dated. It had lasted all of six weeks and was the longest relationship she'd had since Nicole. She'd given up on finding love years ago and had simply quit looking. Besides, no one compared to the love of her life, the woman she still loved with all of her heart and despised at the same time. "Tracey's girlfriend is also in the Coast Guard. She's at sea on a cutter ship at the moment. I've seen her a few times when she's visited."

"Well, that stinks," Caitlin uttered. "I really think she likes you."

"We're good friends. Actually, Greg is a good friend of mine too. We all look out for each other." She paused before they went into the house. "Caitlin, I haven't dated anyone in a while and there hasn't been anyone serious since your mother. I just thought you should know that."

"Do you still love her?"

"I always will," Finley sighed.

Chapter 7

July 4th arrived in the middle of the following week. Finley, Greg, and Tracey were all on standby for the next forty-eight hours.

"I can't believe you talked me into throwing a party," Finley mumbled as she sprayed some dirt off the small deck outback with the water hose.

"If you recall, it wasn't really my idea. It was your friends'."

"Touché." Finley grinned, squirting her with water.

"Hey! What was that for?" Caitlin squealed.

Finley shrugged and laughed.

"Care for some company?" Tracey said, coming up the path along the side of the house. A pretty, Asian-American woman was walking next to her.

"Hey, Lillian! I didn't know you'd be here." Finley smiled, giving her a hug when they walked up.

"I got liberty at the last minute and decided to drive up. I have to go back tomorrow though."

Finley looked around for Caitlin, who had gone into the house with the neighbor's daughter to dry off and start putting some of the food together. "Come inside, there's someone I want you to meet."

Tracey and Lillian followed her through the open doorway.

"Caitlin, this is Boatswains Mate Petty Officer Third

Class Lillian Taka, Tracey's girlfriend."

"Oh, the one on the ship," Caitlin said, smiling. "It's nice to meet you."

"Lillian, this is my daughter, Caitlin."

"I've heard all about you too," Lillian replied, wiggling her eye brows. "Something about going on a search and rescue call."

"Yes! Oh, my God, it was so much fun!"

Lillian laughed. "I wish my job was that exciting."

"Are you kidding me? You patrol for drug smuggling boats and refugees," Tracey retorted. "All I do is hoist her ass in and out of the water," she added with a grin, nodding towards Finley.

"Yeah, yeah." Finley rolled her eyes and laughed. "Come on, you showed up early, so I'm putting you to work," she said, explaining that she needed an extra hand with the grill, and the girls could use some assistance on the dessert cake recipe they'd found online.

"I'll stay in here with the girls, if you want to go outside with her," Lillian said, knowing baking wasn't exactly Tracey's forte.

*

"I'm glad Lillian is here with you," Finley mumbled, as she basted the chicken breasts that were cooking on the grill, with barbecue sauce.

"Why is that?" Tracey asked, turning the shrimp and vegetable skewers.

"Caitlin thought you and I were dating," Finley replied.

"Seriously?" Tracey laughed. "Um…not likely."

"Exactly."

"So, that's why she knew about Lillian."

Finley nodded.

"What about her other mother?" Tracey bit the corner of her mouth and looked at her friend. "You don't have to talk about it if you don't want to."

Finley shrugged. "There's not much to say really. We were high school sweethearts that I thought were madly in love, until seven years ago when she walked out of my life, taking our daughter with her," Finley sighed. "She's now married to a man."

"Holy shit," Tracey whispered.

"Yep." Finley nodded.

"I see why you don't talk about it. You still love her, don't you?"

"Always," Finley murmured, flipping the chicken.

Tracey patted her on the back. "I need a beer," she laughed.

"I've found that whiskey goes pretty good with that story," Finley replied.

"Even better. I wish we weren't on standby. My luck, I'll have one drink and we'll get called out."

"That's how it usually happens."

"I remember one night about three and half years ago, when I was stationed in Miami. The night I met Lillian. I hadn't been there long, maybe five or six weeks. I had forgotten about being on standby when I went out with a couple of friends. She was on liberty because her ship was in port after three months at sea, and she and her mates were tossing them back. The next thing I know, my phone went off in the middle of the night. I woke up, still three sheets to the wind, with no idea how much I'd drank. Plus, I was naked...on her living room floor," Tracey laughed. "She was passed out beside me."

"Oh, no." Finley smiled and shook her head.

"Yeah, not one of my best moments. I mean it was great, at least what I remember of it anyway." She grinned.

"You didn't go out on the call, did you?"

"No. Of course not. I never answered. As soon as the sun came up, I went to the hospital, puking my guts out, with a hangover from hell. I told them I'd eaten raw oysters the night before, so they gave me a nausea prescription, and wrote me a physician's note saying I was suffering from food poisoning."

"Wow. You went all out," Finley replied.

"I had to. I've never had a bad mark, and I've never made that mistake again. The only good thing that came out of it was my relationship with Lillian," Tracey said, replacing the skewers on the grill with raw ones. "I'm going to take these inside and see how the cake is coming," she added, referring to the skewers that were cooked.

Finley nodded and basted the chicken again. Then, she plopped down in a deck chair and closed her eyes behind her sunglasses, letting her skin soak up the hot sun.

"What's burning?" Tracey asked, stepping back outside a few minutes later.

"Shit!" Finley shrieked, jumping up to check the chicken. Thankfully, some barbecue sauce had dripped down on the burner, and the chicken wasn't on fire.

Tracey laughed. "They're having a blast in there. How long is Caitlin here for?"

"She goes home next week," Finley said, removing the cooked chicken from the grill. "Swimming season starts in October, so she has to be ready for tryouts when school starts next month."

"I forgot you said she was a swimmer."

"Yeah. She's probably going to be better than I was at her age."

"That's awesome. I'm assuming she wants to be a rescue swimmer too."

"I'm not sure. I really want her to go to college, and a swimming scholarship is very possible. I was offered one when I graduated, but with Nicole pregnant, I needed a career right away, not a degree." Finley shrugged. "Anyway, her club coach is trying to get her onto the USA Junior National Team, which will more than likely happen this year. Maybe she'll get a chance at the Olympics one day."

"Do you think that is more successful than what you do every day, saving lives?" Tracey asked.

"No, not exactly. I just want her to do what she wants to do and be her own person. If she came to me tomorrow and said she was done with swimming, I'd never mention it again. If she graduates high school and joins the Coast Guard, I'll be standing proudly beside her in my uniform when she signs up and leaves for boot camp. I'm not really pushing her in any direction. I guess it's more like watching to see which way she goes and offering as much guidance as I can along the way."

"Caitlin is one lucky kid to have you as her mother."

"Thanks," Finley uttered.

*

The party had gone better than expected. Greg and a few others from the base had shown up with a massive box of fireworks, which pretty much turned things into a block party when the neighbors all came outside. Thankfully, no one was called in.

Finley was half asleep on the couch, while sitting up with her feet resting on the coffee table, completely beat from the day. Entertaining people used way more energy than swimming in the ocean, rescuing people. She wondered how some people did this on a weekly basis. At least the house wasn't a wreck. Tracy and Lillian had stayed late to help her and Caitlin clean up.

"I had a lot of fun today," Caitlin said, plopping down next to her with a large piece of layered, red, white, and blue cake, on a plate. It was the last remnants of the creation she'd made with the help of Lillian and the neighbor, and had been a complete hit. It was yellow cake, with a layer of strawberries, a layer of blueberries, and whipped icing. Getting in the spirit of the holiday, they'd also added little American flags on toothpick sticks that Caitlin had found at the party store.

Finley pried one eye open, wondering how the hell the kid was still awake after the long day. *I'm getting old,* she thought as she reached a finger out, swiping some of the icing.

"I have two forks," Caitlin chided, handing her one of them.

Finley smiled and began helping her eat the tasty dessert.

"I'm going to the lap pool in the morning. Do you want to go?" Finley asked. She ran everyday as her cardio workout, then hit the weights afterwards, but she also swam in the lap pool at the local health club multiple times a week. She started taking Caitlin to the lap pool every evening so that she kept her training up while she was away from home. Sometimes, Caitlin went with the neighbor and her daughter, who liked to play tennis at the facility.

"What time are you getting up?" Caitlin asked.

"Oh, I don't know. I might sleep in, so maybe six or six-thirty. If you don't want to go in the morning, I'll still take you in the afternoon or evening as usual."

"It's fine. I'll get up and go with you," Caitlin said, finishing the last of the cake.

Finley watched her get up and carry the plate to the kitchen, tossing it in the trash. *I'm going to miss you so much,* she thought, sighing audibly.

"What's wrong?" Caitlin asked, walking back into the living room, where she stopped in front of the couch.

"Nothing. I'm just tired. Are you ready for bed? I think I'm going to call it a night."

"I probably should go to bed since I'm getting up at the crack of dawn to kick your butt in the pool!" Caitlin teased.

Finley raised a brow. "You've raced me five times, and if I recall correctly, I've won them all."

"Whatever. That's because you wear fins!"

"I train in all of my gear, not just fins. Therefore, I'm weighed down. Plus, I'm not a spring chicken anymore. You should be faster than me," Finley quipped.

Caitlin crossed her arms and pinned her with a look that had Nicole written all over it.

Finley smiled and stood up. "Your mother used to look at me the same way when she knew I was right," she said. "I'll make a deal with you. If you can beat me one time at fifty meters while I'm in my gear, I'll take it off and we'll go head to head for another fifty meters."

"Deal," Caitlin said, holding out her hand.

Finley shook her hand.

Then, Caitlin wrapped her in a bear hug. "I love you, Mom."

"I love you too, kiddo."

"I don't want to go home next week."

I don't want you to either. "You have to get ready for school, and you said it yourself, if you want to make captain your freshman year, you have to be at your best at tryouts."

"I know," Caitlin sighed. "I just don't want to see Dave. I do miss Mom a lot, even though we fight."

"That's part of growing up. Grammy and I used to argue too. I think all teenagers go through a stage where they are at war with their parents. It'll pass."

"What about Dave? He's not going anywhere."

"No, but he's not going to run your life either. I want you to respect him like you do all adults. If he crosses the line, you let me know. He's your mother's problem, not yours."

"Okay." Caitlin nodded with a thin smile.

Chapter 8

The next morning, Finley was up before the sun and already in the kitchen, drinking coffee, when she heard a bloodcurdling scream from Caitlin.

"Mom!"

"What's wrong?" Finley shouted as she jumped up from the dining table, racing towards the stairs.

"Mom! Hurry!" Caitlin screamed.

"I'm here!" Finley yelled as she burst through the door of her spare bedroom.

Caitlin was standing next to the bed in her t-shirt and panties, crying her eyes out. Finley moved to her. That's when she noticed the red spots on the sheet.

Oh, no. Why now? Nicole is so much better for this than me. Finley ran her hand through her hair. "It's okay. You're not dying. You just started your period. All girls go through this," she murmured, wrapping her arm around Caitlin's shoulders. "Come on, let's go to the bathroom and get you cleaned up. Did they teach you anything about this in school? Health class or something?"

"A little. Most of the kids made fun of it."

"Great," Finley whispered to herself.

"Mom told me about it though."

Oh, thank God. Nicole, you're an angel!

"So, you know what to do then?"

"Yes and no. My stomach hurts bad like someone punched me. Is that part of it?"

"Unfortunately, yes. Those are called cramps." Finley looked through the cabinet in the spare bathroom for supplies. She grabbed the bottle of Advil, a tampon, and a pad. "Okay, so take two of these about every four to six hours for the pain. It will probably last about two days—"

"The whole thing?"

"No, the cramps. The whole thing is usually five to seven days," Finley replied flatly.

"That sucks."

"Yep. So, anyway, get in the shower and get cleaned up. When you get out, you put one of these on your panties to soak everything up. Just make sure you check it every couple of hours. There's also these for when you get older," she said, pointing to the tampon. "They kind of go up in there, so if you're not sexually active, which you're not right?" *Oh, God, please say no.*

"Eww, gross. No!"

Thank God! "Okay, well, when you get older...*much* older, you can use these. They're a pain in the butt, but much cleaner to deal with. Any questions?" Finley asked, finally meeting her eyes.

Caitlin shook her head no.

"All right. Well, I'll leave you to it. Call me if you need anything. We'll put off our swim race until this is over."

"I leave in six days and you said this will last seven."

"Five to seven," Finley clarified. "It may only last two or three days since it's your first time. Let's see how things go." She closed the door and let out a heavy breath. Then, she trotted back down the stairs to her cold cup of

88

coffee. "Wonderful," she grumbled, snatching her phone from the counter.

It was nearly seven a.m., surely Nicole would be up, getting ready for work. Finley stepped out onto the back deck and scrolled through her phone. Nicole came up by name, with no picture. She'd refused to use her married name, so she left the last name blank. The sun had already crested the coastline and was slowly rising in the sky, painting everything in a bright orange glow. Finley watched a seagull fly over as she listened to the phone ringing.

"Hello?" Nicole answered, groggily.

"Hey. I need to tell you something?" Finley stated.

"Finley?" she questioned, sounding a little more awake.

"Who is it?" A deep male voice called.

"It's nothing. Go back to bed," Nicole said.

Finley heard rustling, then the click of a door. "What time is it?" Nicole whispered.

"It's after seven. Shouldn't you be headed to work?" *Shouldn't he? Don't you people work?*

I took the day off to go with Dave. We're putting his mother in a nursing home today."

She's still alive? She must be a hundred, Finley thought.

"Are you there?" Nicole asked. "Why are you calling me so early? Is Caitlin okay?"

"Yes. She's fine, but she started her period."

"Oh, no."

"Oh, yes."

"Is she all right?"

"I just said she was fine. She told me you talked to her about everything."

"I did. A few of her friends started theirs last year. So, I made sure she knew what it was and everything."

"I think it freaked her out a little bit, and she's dealing with cramps, so that made it worse."

"Poor baby. I'm glad it finally came. I was starting to worry."

"I was a late bloomer too. Mine started around the same age, I think. Anyway, I just wanted to let you know. I'll tell her to call you later, so you can go back to sleep."

"No. I'd like to talk to her now, if that's okay. I'm up anyway."

"I'll see if she's out of the shower," Finley said, walking back into the house. She put the phone on hold and meandered up the stairs. "Caitlin?" she called.

"Yes, ma'am?" Caitlin answered, coming out of the spare bedroom with the sheets in a ball. She was freshly showered and dressed in a pair of loose, cotton shorts and a t-shirt.

"I would've done all of that. It's not a big deal. Your mom's on the phone."

"Did you tell her?" Caitlin asked.

"Yes."

Caitlin nodded and grabbed the phone. Finley took the sheets to the laundry room, stuffing them into the washer as Caitlin headed down the stairs. "You're growing up too fast for me, kid," she whispered, shaking her head.

*

Four days later, Finley was sitting at the dining room table, drinking coffee and eating a loaded, egg-white omelet with a side of turkey bacon, when Caitlin sat down in front of her own identical breakfast plate.

"You look chipper this morning," Finley said.

"The red devil is gone!"

Finley laughed. Is that what you're calling it?"

Caitlin nodded between bites of food.

Finley grinned.

"Can we go do our swim race today?"

Finley bit her lower lip as she thought. She was on standby for the next two days and had planned to spend as much time with Caitlin as possible. "I don't see why not," she replied. "You'd better eat another omelet though."

"Why?" Caitlin asked, swiping an extra piece of bacon from Finley's plate.

"Hey, that's my protein, pal! Get your own!"

Caitlin ate it like a cartoon, chomp, chomp, chomp. Then, she smiled.

Finley shook her head. "Do you want to go this morning, or wait until the afternoon?"

"Either is fine with me."

"All right. We'll let our food settle, then head over there."

*

The fifty-meter, Olympic-sized lap pool at the health club was nearly empty at eight in the morning. All of the morning swimmers had gone to work already, leaving the older, retired people, who congregated at the other end, swimming slow and steady laps, and doing water aerobics.

"Have you ever done yoga?" Caitlin asked, as she set her towel down.

Finley was already putting her gear on nearby. "No," she answered. "Yoga wasn't a big thing when I was younger, so I never really got into it. Why?"

91

"Coach McAdams, my club coach, told me to start doing yoga. He said it helps stretch out your body. Lillian told me she does yoga twice a day and she does Pilates when she's ashore."

"Oh, really?" Finley tried to think of Tracey ever talking about Pilates.

"Yeah. That's probably why she has a great body."

Finley raised an eyebrow.

"Mom goes to a yoga class four or five times a week, and she also goes to a spin class once a week. She used to do Pilates, but Dave said she was exercising too much."

Finley nodded, not wanting to get into a conversation about him. "If your coach thinks it's a good idea, why not give it a try. You can always stop if you don't like it. You'll never know whether or not it works for you, or if you even like it, if you don't try it."

"I know. I'm thinking of going to yoga with Mom when I get home."

"That's a good idea. I think she'd like that," Finley said, pulling on her fins. "All right. So, do you want to go off the side like a block, or get in the water and push off the wall?" she asked.

"Off the side is fine."

"Are you ready?" Finley asked, checking her gear one last time.

"Yes, ma'am," Caitlin replied, getting into position.

Finley bent down, putting her hands on the edge of the pool. "On your mark…get set…Go!" she yelled.

They dove in at the same time. Finley surfaced first and Caitlin swam underwater a little longer. Finley swam fast, one hand over the other, taking little peeks next to her on every other stroke. Caitlin was close, about even with her fins, which did propel Finley a little further with each stroke. However, her gear did slow her down.

After a quick peek to see how close they were, Finley backed off a little, allowing Caitlin to get even with her. At that point, Caitlin realized she had a chance and kicked it into another gear, swimming as hard and as fast as she could. When they reached the wall, Caitlin touched first, with Finley right behind her. Less than a second separated the two of them.

"Yes!" Caitlin cheered, smiling brightly like a little kid.

"You got me," Finley replied with a grin.

The people on the other end of the pool clapped when they got out. Finley smiled and waved. Then, she began taking off her gear, and stripping down to the bathing suit she'd worn under her wetsuit. "Are you sure you want to take me on?" she asked.

"Oh, please. I just smoked you. I've got this," Caitlin poked her chest out like a prized rooster.

"We'll see, kid," Finley laughed and sat on the edge, giving Caitlin time to catch her breath after swimming her heart out.

"I'm ready when you are," Caitlin said. "Or do you need more time?"

Finley grinned. "I'm good. Are we starting the same way?"

"Sure."

Finley bent down again, putting her hands on the edge of the pool. Caitlin mimicked her position. "On your mark…get set…Go!" Finley shouted.

They both dove in. Caitlin stayed under much longer, giving her a bit of an edge on her mother, but Finley was fast. They were neck and neck, nearly stroke for stroke, until Finley pushed ahead for the last quarter of the pool. They touched the wall at nearly the same time.

"Oh, my God," Caitlin gasped. "Who won? Was it me?"

Finley shrugged and looked to the other end of the pool.

"Too close to call!" the seniors doing water aerobics shouted.

"I guess it's a tie then," Finley said.

"Man, you swim fast," Caitlin mumbled, still trying to catch her breath.

"So do you, kiddo!" Finley beamed, wrapping her arm around Caitlin's shoulders.

*

Two days later, Finley stood at the airport in her flight suit. She was scheduled to go back on nights, so she was seeing Caitlin's plane off, then heading to the air station for the shift change.

"Can I come back for my holiday break?" Caitlin asked.

"We'll see. That's a long way off, and I have another transfer coming up. If nothing else, I'll come up and see you at Grammy's."

Caitlin nodded and asked, "Where do you think you'll get sent this time?"

"I don't know."

"Do they send you back to bases you've been at before?"

"Sure they do," Finley answered. "I have a little bit of seniority, so I'll be sent where I am needed the most, more than likely, but I also have some choices."

"I wish they would send you back to Charleston," Caitlin mumbled.

"Charleston doesn't have an airbase, that's why I'm not there. I started there because I was part of an aircrew on a cutter ship."

"Can't that happen again?"

"No," Finley sighed. *At least not like that. I want to be closer to you, Caitlin. You just don't know how hard that is for me.* "They only assign new swimmers to cutter duty because there isn't a lot of action. They fly a lot, patrolling the water, but they don't do a lot of rescues. I have to be at a high volume base."

Caitlin nodded.

"I promise to see you more. Whether it's you coming to stay wherever I am, or me coming up there to stay with Grammy."

"I'm going to miss you so much. I'll send you a picture of me in my uniform as soon as I get it," she said excitedly.

"I can't wait." Finley smiled. *Nicole is going to love that,* she thought, shaking her head. "Keep me updated on your swim meets too."

"I will. Mom always videos them."

"I know. She sends them to me."

"She does?"

"Yes."

"I never knew that," Caitlin said. "I mean, I know she emails you, but I didn't realize she sent you stuff like that."

"Your mom's not a robot, Caitlin. She does have some compassion, or at least she used to. I know things aren't easy right now, but you have four more years until you graduate. Then, you're off on your own. Hopefully, at college."

"You didn't go to college."

"No, but your mother did, and I want you to go too. I could've gone, but I turned down my scholarship to take care of you and her."

"Yeah, then she ruined our lives."

"Caitlin…" Finley sighed.

"I know, I know. But, look at where you are now. You love what you do, and you make a difference, saving lives. What is a college degree going to do for me?"

"It can do a lot of things, if you let it. Listen, you don't need to decide anything today, but I want you to work hard and get good grades. If you love swimming, then keep doing what you love. Train hard, work hard, and you'll achieve your dreams," Finley said, wrapping her in a hug. "I didn't know I wanted to join the Coast Guard until right before I graduated. I was supposed to go to the University of South Carolina. Anyway, what I'm saying is, don't lose focus on you. I want you to grow up and be Caitlin. Not Finley or Nicole, or anyone else. Be your own person and make your life what you want it to be. You're so young and you have so much ahead of you."

Caitlin smiled. "You sound just like Mom telling me not to worry about boys until I'm older. She gives me the same talk, but it's about sex and getting pregnant. She told me to wait until I am out of college, or at least settled in the life that I want."

"She's absolutely right," Finley agreed. At least she and Nicole were on the same page when it came to their daughter. "You better go catch your plane," she added, checking her watch. "This security officer will take you through security and down to your gate."

"Okay," Caitlin said.

"Check in at the desk when you get there. Your flight leaves in thirty minutes."

Caitlin wrapped her arms around Finley. "I love you, Mom."

"I love you too, kiddo."

Finley wiped away a few tears as she watched Caitlin walk through the security checkpoint, until she could no longer see her in the terminal. Then, she headed to the lobby to watch the screen until she knew the flight had taken off. Once it said departed, Finley picked up her phone.

"Hey, Mom. Caitlin's plane is in the air. Can you call Nicole for me and let her know?"

"Sure. I thought you were talking on the phone with her now," her mother replied.

"I was, but that's because Caitlin was here with me. Now, she's gone, so..."

Jackie Morris heard the sadness in her daughter's voice. "You're never going to let her go, are you?"

Finley had no idea how to answer that. She'd tried time and time again to let Nicole go, to hate her and push her out of her life, but they were connected forever through Caitlin. That lifeline always seemed to keep them within arm's length, no matter what. "I've dated, if that's what you're asking."

"You know what I mean," Jackie replied. "Anyway, how did everything go?"

"You mean with Caitlin here? It was great. She got to go out on a call with me, which blew her mind."

"Really? I bet that was exciting."

"Yeah. I really enjoyed having her here. I feel like I've missed so much of her growing up these past seven years."

"Well, you have, honey. But, it wasn't on your own accord, and you know that."

"I know. I miss her already," Finley said, walking out of the airport. "Things aren't going too great for her at home."

"What's wrong?"

"I guess Nicole's marriage isn't wedded bliss after all."

"Well, I could've told you that. He's an absolute ass and she's stupid for marrying him in the first place."

"It is what it is, Mom. She made her choices, now she has to live with them," she said, getting into her SUV.

"We both know her mother made them for her."

"Well, she allowed it!" Finley snapped.

"I know that," Jackie countered.

"I really don't want to talk about Nicole or her marriage. I just sent my little girl back to that mess, not knowing when I will see her again."

"Have you thought about taking Caitlin fulltime?"

"What? You mean like full custody?"

"Sure. Why not?"

Finley shook her head and pulled out into the airport traffic. "That would never happen. First, Nicole would never allow it. Second, my schedule is too chaotic. I had to leave her alone in the house or with my neighbor as it was, and that was only for a few weeks. Plus, my transfer is coming up. Who the hell knows where I'll wind up this time." Finley sighed, "No, she's better off where she is."

"I disagree with you."

Finley rolled her eyes. "I need to go, Mom. I have to be ready for shift change in twenty minutes."

"You're back on nights already?"

"Every three weeks," Finley replied.

"Be safe out there. I love you," Jackie said.

"I love you, too. Don't forget to call Nicole," Finley said, before tossing her phone into the passenger seat. The short drive around to the backside of the airport where the Coast Guard Air Station was located, had taken less than five minutes. She'd planned to use the other fifteen to try and forget how sad she felt knowing Caitlin wouldn't be there waiting when she got home.

*

"Is everything okay?" Greg asked, noticing Finley was less talkative than usual, which wasn't saying much. They'd just finished their shift and were sitting in a coffee shop, eating pancakes.

"We need to stop coming here," she replied with a mouthful of food. "I'm going to get fat."

Greg laughed. "Oh, please. You get whole-wheat pancakes topped with organic fruit and low-fat granola, and put a drop of natural honey on it for syrup. I think you'll be fine. Besides, you run like a hamster on a wheel. That has to burn off the little bit of excess calories you might be eating right now."

Finley rolled her eyes and took another sizeable bite.

"Sorry I'm late. My car wouldn't start. Apparently, I left my headlights on all night," Tracey mumbled, sliding into the booth next to Finley.

"Really? I'm surprised no one noticed and said anything," Greg replied.

"Seriously? You think anyone gives a shit?" Tracey retorted, waving the waitress over to the table.

"If anyone noticed, it would be security because the parking lot is on the other side of the hangars. The tower might be able to see it, but their backs are to that area," Finley stated.

"I'll just have a coffee, black," Tracey said, placing her order.

Greg raised an eyebrow.

"What?" Tracey questioned. "I can't eat when we come off the night shift. I have to sleep first."

"Not me, I'm usually starving," Finley said.

"Me too," Greg added. "Have fun, ladies. I'm going to hit the gym before heading home. I'll see you tonight."

Finley waved and Tracey said goodbye as she moved around to the opposite side of the booth. "Is Caitlin leaving soon?" she asked.

"She actually left yesterday."

"Really? Why didn't you say anything?"

"Nothing much to say."

"Well, she was a joy to be around. I hope I get to see her again."

"She won't be back here. My transfer is coming up."

"I still have another year. I'm hoping to go back to Miami next, but I don't know since I was just there," Tracey replied. "What are you going to do?"

"I don't know. I still have a little time before I need to turn in my preference, and I've been offered an instructor position at the rescue swimmer school."

"Wow. Congratulations. That's a big decision," Tracey exclaimed.

"Thanks," she murmured. "I don't know if I want to come out of the field for three years. That's a long time, especially when I've been at some of the most active posts for more than half of my time in service."

"It might seem like a step back, but it's a great opportunity for someone with your skill level. Look at all of the recruits you'll be sharing your knowledge with."

"That's true. I have a lot to think about," she said, looking at her bill. "It's in Charleston, where my family is, including Caitlin and her mother."

"Ah, I see the hesitation." Tracey nodded. "I take it you and she don't get along."

"It's not that easy. We actually don't speak to each other at all. When Caitlin was here, I talked to her on the phone for the first time in seven years. Everything sort of came flooding back. I thought I had let go, or was at least headed in that direction."

"Women…" Tracey muttered, shaking her head. "They will fuck you up."

"No kidding," Finley laughed. "Honestly, I would love being closer to Caitlin, but giving up three years in the field is difficult, especially when I'll be cleared to retire in seven years."

"Do you think you'll do more than that?"

"Oh, I'm sure. My plan was to go as close to twenty years as I could in the field, then transfer and finish out my career as an instructor at the swim school, doing twenty-five full years of active duty in service."

"Well, if you made a plan, why not stick to it?" Tracey questioned.

"You make it sound so easy. Maybe you're in the wrong career. You should be a therapist or something, instead of a Flight Mechanic," Finley laughed. "Come on, let's get out of here. I'm tired," she added, tossing a ten dollar bill on the table.

Chapter 9

Three weeks into the month of August, Finley had just finished a long shift, where she'd rescued multiple survivors from three different calls. She'd had a busy day and was completely worn out, but the blinking light on her phone, indicating she had received an email, cheered her up. She quickly went through the process to open her mail. Two emails were waiting for her. She touched the line to open the first one.

From: NWetherby@mail.com
Subject: Caitlin 1st swim practice

Finley,

Here is the video from Caitlin's first formal practice with the swim team. They haven't narrowed the roster or anything yet, but I thought you'd like to see her swimming in the Annandale pole. Looks so much like you out there. Anyway, the season officially starts next month.

Nicole

Finley swiped the button to play the one minute video. She smiled, watching Caitlin skim through the water like a dolphin. The large, red and white Annandale High sign was visible on the far wall. It brought back memories of the countless hours Finley had spent in that pool, with Nicole Wetherby in the stands watching, cheering her on, and waiting to hang out when she was finished.

After watching it play a second time, Finley closed the video. She thought about replying, but there wasn't much to say, at least not to Nicole. She quickly moved onto the second email.

From: swimmerCFM@mail.com
Subject: check this out

Hey,

I'm sure Mom won't send this to you, so I will! I love you and I miss you. When are you coming up to Grammy's? Can't wait to show you in person!

Caitlin

Finley scrolled down to the picture at the bottom. Caitlin was dressed in the dark blue slacks, light blue blouse, and dark blue garrison cap of her Air Force Junior ROTC cadet uniform. Her Airman rank insignia was on both of the shirt lapels and the name Morris was proudly displayed on the front right chest.

Tracey noticed Finley smiling from ear to ear and walked over. "What has you all happy? Is someone sexting you?" she laughed.

Finley raised an eyebrow and turned her phone around.

"Oh, wow. Look at your mini-me," Tracey exclaimed. "You should see your face right now. You're beaming like one proud momma."

Finley chuckled. "Oh, I absolutely love it. She looks so grown up. But, I'm actually pretty giddy because I know her mother must hate every minute of this."

"Really? She hates the military that much, or is it you?"

Finley shrugged. "She has no reason to hate me, but her mother despises the military, mostly because of me." She shook her head. "Oh, talk about hatred, that woman hates my guts."

Tracey giggled. "She sounds lovely."

"No kidding," Finley laughed.

"I'll see you in a few days," Tracey said, tossing her bag full of dirty flight suits over her shoulder. "Enjoy your standby weekend."

"Did you take time off to finally do your laundry?"

"No, smartass," Tracey growled with a smile. "I'm heading down to Miami for Lillian's birthday. Her ship is coming in tomorrow and she'll have liberty all weekend."

"Have fun," Finley called as Tracey walked away. She scrolled back to the top of the email and hit reply.

Caitlin,

Love the picture! You so look so grown up! I'm very proud of you. Remember, anytime you have on a service uniform, wear it proudly with your shoulders squared and your chin held high. I can't wait to see some ribbons on it at the end of the school year.

Also, your mom sent me the video of swim practice. Looking good, kiddo! I miss you and I love you. I'll see you soon.

Mom

*

Finley's head had barely hit the pillow on Saturday night, when her phone began ringing loudly. She'd spent the entire day out by the river reading a book and soaking up the sun. She was beat and the last thing she wanted to do was go out on a call. She rolled over, grabbing the phone and swiping to answer at the same time.

"Morris."

"Chief, we need a swimmer. We have a missing person from a cruise ship and need another bird in the air," said the Operations Duty Officer who was on shift.

"I'm on the way," she replied, ending the call. She quickly splashed some cold water on her face, gargled some mouthwash, and pulled on a dark blue t-shirt, before stepping into her flight suit. Within two minutes, she was out the door.

Navigating the streets in the middle of the night was much easier than the daytime. Merritt Island wasn't big by any means, but it was cram packed with people in the summer, mostly tourists. It took her all of five minutes to get to the air station. She showed her ID to the guard at the gate and drove around to the parking lot behind the main hangar.

"I figured I'd see you," Greg said, getting out of his car a few spaces away.

"I couldn't go all weekend without seeing your scruffy face," she teased.

"Shit," he squeaked, reaching into his flight bag for the electric razor he kept for emergencies. The Coast Guard was pretty easygoing, unlike the strict demands of most branches. However, getting caught with facial hair would get him a reprimand.

Finley checked the weather on her phone, while Greg shaved his face as they walked towards the hangar.

"Who the hell jumps off a cruise ship? That seems to be happening more and more lately," he mumbled.

Finley shrugged as she pulled open the door.

Lieutenant Commander James Kline, the Operations Duty Officer for the night, was standing outside of the dispatch office, waiting for their arrival. "6529 is bingo and heading in," he said, referring to the other helo that was operated by the aircrew who was currently on shift. "We need to get you guys in the air now. As far as we know, the woman was reported missing less than an hour ago."

"Roger," Greg said. He and Finley rushed to their lockers to prepare for the flight. He began putting his survival harness on, while she changed into her swimmer gear.

"Nice night for a flight," stated another aircrew member as he tightened his survival harness and closed his locker.

"You're flying with us tonight, D?" Greg asked, looking at the young Flight Mechanic.

"Yes, sir," Deacon beamed.

Greg laughed and shook his head. "This ought to be fun."

"It always is, brother," Deacon grinned as he headed over to the helo to start his preflight checklist.

"How is he always so wired?" Finley mumbled, grabbing her mask, snorkel, and fins, before closing her locker.

"He drinks those energy drinks like water," Greg replied, walking with her to the helo.

"We're fueled and ready to go," Deacon said, as they stepped closer. "The emergency equipment is all accounted for," he added, looking at Finley.

Greg and Finley completed their own preflight checks, along with the co-pilot who would be accompanying them. Once they were finished, they went into the operations office for a last minute briefing before taking flight, where they were given the approximate coordinates of the fall location, the time, wind speed and direction, and sea data.

*

Finley and Deacon were tethered to the helo with gunner belts as they scanned the water with night vision goggles through the open cabin door. Both of the Coast Guard Search and Rescue helicopters were scanning grids along the path of the current, and thirty miles apart. Because of a lapse in the last time the woman was seen and when she was reported missing, no one knew exactly when she went into the water.

"Search and Rescue 6516, Search and Rescue 6529...Sector Merritt Island. We have just been updated by Paradise Cruise Line. The victim was seen going over the rail on closed circuit video at 1200. Over."

"Sector...6529. Copy," the second helo radioed.

"Sector...6516. Can we get the coordinates of the ship at the time of the fall? Over." Greg said.

The dispatcher quickly replied with the latitude and longitude information.

"6529...6516. Stay on course. We're going to backtrack towards the last known position. Over," Greg radioed to the other helo as he changed course.

"6516...6529. Copy," the other pilot replied.

"She's been in the water for nearly two hours. Even if she wasn't drunk, that's a long time to tread water," Deacon uttered.

"At this point, we're looking at a body retrieval," Finley said.

"Yeah. I'd be surprised if we found her alive," Greg added as they flew over the position where the woman had gone overboard. He took the helo down to thirty feet over the fairly calm seas. "I'm going to stay on this path and follow the current," he stated.

*

Finley and Deacon scanned the water back and forth for the next half hour. She finally began scanning further out from their position. Without the aid of night vision, they were surrounded in total darkness, except for the illumination from the gauges and sensors in the cockpit.

"Sector...6516. We are five minutes out from bingo fuel. Over," Greg radioed. "Crew, prepare to depart for refueling," he said.

"Greg, check your three o'clock, about four hundred yards out," Finley said.

He didn't have binoculars to see that far out, so he banked the helo to the right and headed towards the area she was referring to.

"6516…Sector. Copy on bingo. Return for refuel. Over."

"Sector…6516. Hold off on the refuel. We may have a visual. Over."

"Mark. Mark. Mark," Finley yelled, tossing a blinking buoy in the water as they flew over the body that was floating face down.

Greg circled back around and hovered over the blinking light, thirty feet up. "Sector…6516. We have located the survivor. Deploying swimmer. Be advised, we are at bingo fuel. Over."

Finley sat on the edge on the open cabin door with the hoist attached to her harness.

"Swimmer is ready," Deacon said.

"Deploy swimmer. Let's make this quick, guys," Greg said.

Finley checked her harness when the hoist lifted her off the ground. She gave Deacon the thumbs up and he began to lower her down.

"Swimmer is in the water. Swimmer is okay. Swimmer is away," he said as Finley went into the water and raised her hand to indicate everything was good. Then, she unclipped the hoist line and swam over to the woman.

When she reached the lifeless woman, Finley rolled her over, pulling her face from the water. Her motionless eyes were wide open. She checked for a pulse, knowing she wouldn't find one. She softly ran her hand over the woman's eyelids, pushing them closed.

"6516…Rescue Swimmer. Be advised, survivor is DOA. Repeat: DOA. Deploy litter. Over."

"Swimmer…6516. Copy," Greg replied.

Deacon attached the litter to the hoist and lowered it down to the water. Everyone watched in silence as Finley put the woman's body into the floating stretcher and connected the straps that would hold her head, torso, arms, and legs in place. Then, she gave the thumbs up signaling she was ready. Deacon hoisted the litter out of the water slowly and pulled it inside the helo, before sending the hoist line back down to retrieve Finley.

When Finley was back in the helo, she checked the woman once more for a pulse, but she was long gone. "Alert: zero. Confirmed DOA," she radioed with a sigh.

"Sector Merritt Island...Search and Rescue 6516. Be advised, we are en route. Three minutes past bingo fuel. Survivor is DOA. Repeat: DOA. Alert: zero. Over," Greg radioed.

"6516...Sector. Copy."

Finley stared through the window at the stars in the cloudless sky. The moon was only a tiny sliver in the distance. Her eyes slowly fell on the lifeless woman in the basket. It wasn't the first time she'd retrieved a dead body, and she'd had a handful of survivors die on her in flight over the years, but each time it reminded her how quickly life could be taken away.

*

When the helo landed, all of the service members on the base were standing outside with their caps in their hands, watching silently as Finley and Deacon unloaded the litter. An ambulance was parked nearby with the lights off. The two EMTs waited patiently to take the woman's body to the local hospital for official purposes. Finley and Deacon worked with the EMTs to transfer her from the litter to the stretcher. Then, they backed away as the EMTs

111

loaded her into the ambulance and checked her vitals one final time, before covering her with a thin white sheet.

Finley let out a long breath as the ambulance drove away silently. She hated that part of the job. No matter what the circumstance, it never got any easier.

"Do you think that woman jumped?" Deacon asked.

"I don't know," she replied. "I didn't see any visible injuries when I looked her over."

"What do you think makes people do it? You know, commit suicide? And on a vacation at that?"

Finley shrugged. "No idea, D. I guess they give up and let go of life."

Deacon didn't reply as he began his post flight inspection.

Finley flattened the litter and stowed it away, before doing her post flight check. Then, she completed her paperwork and signed out.

"I'm going over to Dunkin Donuts. You want to go?" Greg asked, catching up to her.

"Really? A doughnut at four a.m.?" She raised an eyebrow.

"I don't want to go home."

"Me either," she sighed.

"Come on, I'm buying." He grinned like a cartoon character.

"All right, but you're going running with me later."

"Deal," he laughed.

"Aren't you going to ask Deacon and Brian?" she said, referring to the flight mechanic and co-pilot who had flown with them.

"Deacon's had enough sugar to give a horse diabetes, and Brian has a new baby at home. This was his first standby shift since they brought the baby home."

"Oh, that's right. I bet he's tired. I remember those days…and nights," she murmured, thinking back to when Caitlin was a new baby. She and Nicole had also had their hands full, learning the ropes of parenting a newborn together.

*

Halfway through a box of doughnuts and two cups of coffee, Finley leaned back in the booth, staring at the sun rising over the parking lot, painting everything in an orange glow.

"How long have you been a Coastie?" she asked.

"Coming up on ten years. You?"

"Almost thirteen and a half," she replied, sipping her coffee. "If you could go be an instructor at the flight school for a few years, would you do it?"

"You mean like between posts?"

"Something like that."

"I don't know. I think it takes a lot of patience, and I'm more of a hands on kind of person. What about you? Would you go be an instructor at the swimmer school?"

"I definitely want to at some point in my career. Those men and women broke me down and built me back up into the person I am today. I was just a kid back then."

"I think you'd be great at it. I've definitely learned a lot just by working with you," he said, grabbing another doughnut out of the box. "What made you bring this up?"

"Just thinking about the future," she muttered. "You're going to have a hell of a time keeping up with me if you keep eating those things," she laughed.

"Who said we were running today?"

"Actually, you can go swimming with me instead, if you want."

Greg shook his head. "I could never be a rescue swimmer," he mumbled, closing the box.

*

Later that afternoon, Finley was half asleep on the couch when the local news came on. She heard the word cruise ship and immediately opened her eyes.

"The forty-five year old woman, identified as Colleen Davis, who died tragically after falling overboard from the Centurion, *a cruise ship owned and operated by Paradise Cruise Lines, may not have been the victim of a tragic suicide as first reported. Authorities haven't commented beyond telling us that they have reason to believe foul play was involved.*

The Centurion *was on the last leg of a cruise through the Caribbean from New Orleans to Boston and Ms. Davis had been accompanied by her boyfriend. She was reported missing early Sunday morning, and her body was later recovered by a Coast Guard Search and Rescue helicopter. We will keep you updated as we learn more,"* the news anchor said.

"Holy shit," Finley whispered.

Chapter 10

A couple of weeks later, Finley was called into the office of the Command Master Chief when her shift ended. She removed her ball cap and sighed. She knew what he wanted. He needed an answer on the transfer to the swim school. An answer she wasn't ready to give him.

"I saw on the news where that woman from the cruise ship was pushed by her boyfriend," he said shaking his head. "I hope they fry his ass."

Finley smiled in agreement. She'd been surprised to learn what had actually happened as well.

"Did you make a decision on the instructor position?" he asked.

"Not yet. I'm still thinking about it," she said honestly.

"What's holding you back?"

"I'm not sure I want to give up being in the field for three years. I know I can opt out after a year if it's not working out, but I'd never do that. Knowing myself, I'd stick it out, no matter what. Therefore, I need to make sure it's the right path for me to take right now. I've always thought about becoming a swim school instructor. Although, I'd planned on doing it a little later in my career, maybe when I was done in the field, you know?"

"That certainly makes sense. However, just so you know, taking this position isn't a step down, a step back, or a step out the door. It's being offered to you because you're in your prime and there's no one better to challenge and lead the next generation than someone like you."

Finley nodded.

"I don't need to send the transfer up the chain until December, so that gives you a few months. That's taking it down to the wire though, so you'll probably lose your requested choice of posts if you decide not to do it since the post transfers are usually completed two months in advance."

"I know," she said. She'd thought of that as well. The only two bases she'd never been assigned to were Miami and the Bahamas, both of which wouldn't be bad places to live for three years. Still, the idea of putting in for another stint in Savannah to at least be closer to Caitlin if she didn't take the instructor position, had played on her mind. Her choice would be considered, but as a senior ranked rescue swimmer, she'd be placed where she was needed.

*

Finley was walking out of the hangar, towards the parking lot when she noticed a voicemail on her phone that mother had left two hours earlier.

Finley, it's Mom. Call me as soon as you get this message. Love you.

Finley quickly pushed the button to call her, wondering what the urgent message was about. "Hey, Mom. Is everything all right?" she asked as her mother answered.

"Yes. Why wouldn't it be?" Jackie Morris replied.

"You left me a message to call you."

"Caitlin found out today that she's marching in the Veterans Day Parade downtown with the ROTC."

"Oh, really?"

"Yes. I figured Nicole wouldn't let you know in time to take off, which is why I called."

"I'm still at the base, so I'll put in the request for the time off now," Finley replied, turning around and walking back inside the hangar. She quickly said goodbye to her mother and ended the call.

Commander Douglas was in his office when she knocked on the door and walked inside.

"Morris? I thought you'd be gone already. Did everything go okay with the Command Master Chief?"

"Oh, yeah. He had some transfer questions for me. Anyway, I need to put in a request to take off a few days in November. My daughter is marching in the Veterans Day Parade with her high school ROTC unit, and I'd really like to be there."

"That's less than sixty days out," he said, looking at the calendar. "Consider your request granted." He smiled. "These are the kinds of things you don't want to miss. Trust me, I know. Go ahead and fill out the paperwork. I'll sign it now."

"Thanks," she replied.

"Are you going to swing by the training center while you're up there?" he asked nonchalantly.

Finley raised an eyebrow. She had no idea he knew anything about her offer to become an instructor.

"I think it's a great opportunity," he said.

"Thanks," she murmured.

Finley slid into her SUV and pushed the button on her phone to call Caitlin. After ringing a couple of times, the gregarious teen answered.

"Hey, Mom!"

"Hey, kiddo. I hear you're marching in a parade."

"Yep! Our whole unit is. Also, I passed my first advancement test, so now I'm an Airman First Class!"

"Caitlin, that's fantastic! I'm very proud of you."

"I was going to join the drill team, but with swimming, I won't have time for all of the practices. So, I joined the color guard instead. They only practice once a week and it's mostly marching, which we do in class anyway."

"That's cool. Will you be with the color guard at the parade?"

"We have two squads and I'm on the B squad, so probably not."

"Well, no matter where you are in the group, I'll be there watching you," Finley said.

"Are you serious?" Caitlin squealed.

"Yes. I'm coming in sometime the day before, so I was hoping maybe you'd want to come to Grammy's and spend the afternoon with us after the parade."

"Awesome! I can't wait to see you. How long will you be here? I have a swim meet on Monday."

"I have to leave the day after, which is Sunday, in order to be back on shift Monday. But, at least I get to come up and see you."

"That stinks, but I'm excited that you'll be at the parade."

"Do me a favor, kiddo. Don't tell your mother I'm coming up."

"Okay. Between you and me, I think she'd be happy to see you. All Dave does is make her cry."

"Nice," Finley murmured.

"Are you working tonight?" Caitlin asked.

"No, I'm just getting off my shift, actually. I had a pretty long day."

"Did you save anyone?"

"We got called out for a guy on a cargo ship who was having chest pain, so we transported him to the hospital. I didn't have to deploy. We sent the basket down, he got in, and we hoisted him up."

"That's no fun," Caitlin sighed.

Finley laughed. "I just pulled up at home, so I'm going to get off the phone. I love you and I'll see you soon."

"Love you too, Mom."

Finley tucked the phone into her flight bag and headed into the house. She used to love the quiet of coming home, but since Caitlin had stayed with her, she missed the hundreds of questions the kid would ask as soon as she walked inside.

As she meandered up the stairs, she couldn't shake the thought of Nicole being brought to tears by the person who was supposed to love her unconditionally. There was nothing she could do about it. Nicole had chosen that life. She knew why it bothered her, though, and there was nothing she could do about that either. Having Caitlin with her had also stirred up a lot of old feelings and memories that she'd buried deep inside.

*

A few weeks later, Finley moseyed into the hangar, dressed in her flight suit, and ready for the shift change. She hated the adjustment from nights back to days. It had always taken her an extra twenty-four hours for her body to get acclimated to the new sleep pattern. After nearly ten years of doing this every three weeks, she wondered if she'd ever get used to it.

"You look tired," Tracey said, bumping shoulders with her.

"I am," Finley replied with a yawn.

"Here, have some of this." Tracey grinned, handing Finley her large, steamy cup of coffee.

The aroma was a little sweet and nutty, reminding her of hazelnut. Finley took a nice long swallow. Then, she choked and gasped. "What the hell was what?" she croaked, feeling like she'd just drank turbine oil laced with sugar.

"Isn't it good?" Tracey beamed. "This is those Robusta coffee beans from Indonesia I was telling you about. I mixed it with two scoops of Nutella powder and a little bit of milk."

"It's strong, that's for sure, and definitely sweet," Finley stated, looking around for something to chase it with.

Tracey laughed. "It'll wake you right up."

Or give me a heart attack, Finley thought. "This is the stuff you bought from that shop in Miami?"

"Yes."

"Is it even legal?" Finley laughed.

"Of course," Tracey giggled. "It's just a hell of a lot stronger than anything you can buy in the shops around here. They import it."

"What's on the agenda for the day?" Greg asked, stepping up behind them.

"Hey, try this coffee," Finley said, taking the cup from Tracey.

"Why? What's in it?"

"It's just coffee," Tracey replied.

Greg took a sip and grimaced. "Yuck. I'll stick to the crap they brew around here," he said, holding up his Styrofoam cup.

Tracey rolled her eyes and followed Finley out to the helo to do her preflight check, still drinking her coffee.

Finley was about to say something when the call siren rang loudly in the hangar. She and Tracey rushed inside to the ODO office.

"A small plane with a single passenger sent a mayday call with engine failure a few minutes ago. He was fifty miles off of Daytona Beach. Twenty seconds after the mayday, the plane disappeared from radar," CDR. Douglas said.

"Roger," Greg replied. "Saddle-up," he said to the aircrew.

Finley put on her bright red wetsuit, followed by her survival harness and water boots. Then, she grabbed her flight bag, along with her fins, mask, and snorkel.

Tracey was the last person to enter the helo through the cabin door. She quickly pulled it shut and slid into her jump seat.

"Crew ready for takeoff?" Greg asked.

"Roger," Finley replied.

"Cabin door is closed. Ready for takeoff," Tracey said.

Greg manipulated the controls. The helo lifted off the ground with ease and headed towards the Atlantic

Ocean. As soon as dispatch radioed him with the last known coordinates, he programmed them into the flight computer.

Finley listened to the hum of the twin turbine engines and watched the blue water pass by through the window during the short, twenty minute flight.

"Search and Rescue 6516...Sector Merritt Island. The pilot has been recovered by a fishing vessel in the area. Repeat: the pilot has been recovered. Return to base. Over," the dispatcher radioed.

"Sector...6516. Copy. Returning to base," Greg replied.

As soon as they landed, Finley hopped out of the helo with her flight bag. "Well, that was fun," she mumbled.

"No kidding. I'm glad I'm off for the next two days," Tracey replied, checking her watch. She still had nine more hours to go on her shift.

"Might as well not look. It's going to be a long day," Finley added, stowing her gear in her locker, before changing back into her flight suit and heading back outside to do her post flight check.

*

The next evening, Finley walked into her house after a long, boring day at the base with zero call outs. After a shark was reported in the Cocoa Beach area, they did a flyover, but never saw anything. She plopped down on the couch, checking her email on her phone. Nicole had sent three separate videos of Caitlin's swim meet from earlier in the day, which she'd won. Finley watched each of them, then scrolled through her phone to make a call.

"Hey, Mom!" Caitlin answered.

"Hey, kiddo. I just saw the videos of your swim meet. Way to go!"

"Thanks. Our team is leading the points in our division right now."

"That's fantastic. How's everything else going?"

"Fine."

"I don't mean just with school. Your grades are good, right?"

"Yes. I'm pretty sure I'm getting all A's for the first semester. I'll know next week when I get my report card."

"Great. And things at home?"

"The same," Caitlin mumbled. "I can't wait until you come up here in a couple of weeks."

"Me too."

"Were you on shift today?"

"Yep."

"Did you save anyone?"

"Nope. We went looking for a shark that was spotted out on the beach. That was the highlight of my day. What about you? It's Halloween. Are you doing anything exciting?"

"My friend Hannah invited me over to dress up scary and pass out candy, but I stayed home with Mom instead. She and Dave had a huge fight a little while ago."

"Oh, really?"

"Yes. They were supposed to go to the party up at the country club. Mom spent all day with me at the swim meet, and then she took me and Hannah to dinner since Dave was out golfing. When we got home, she didn't feel like going to the party. He flipped out, yelling at her."

"Where is he now?"

"Gone. He stormed out of here, slamming the door. I guess he went to the party."

"That piece of shit doesn't deserve her," she mumbled.

"What? I think your phone is breaking up, Mom."

"I asked, where's your mom?"

"Passing out candy to the trick or treat kids."

Finley shook her head and looked at the clock on the wall. "I'm supposed to be at a party too."

"Why didn't you go?"

"It's a costume party…"

"Well, put on some old, ratty clothes, smear ketchup all over them, and go as a zombie victim. That seems to be the big thing this year. Personally, zombies creep me out," Caitlin said.

"I'll see what I can come up with," Finley laughed.

"Cool. Send me a picture."

"I will. I better get going. I love you, kiddo. I'll see you soon."

"Love you too, Mom."

Finley hung up the phone and went upstairs to search her closet.

*

"Look at what the cat drug in," Tracey exclaimed, pulling her front door open. "It's about time you arrived."

"Yeah, well, some of us had to work today."

"Oh, please. I heard all about your shark hunt. Sounds like I missed a hell of a lot of nothing."

"Pretty much," Finley laughed.

"Oh…I like your costume," Lillian said, giving Finley a hug as she entered the kitchen.

"Me too," said a young woman who was standing next to Lillian. "The Walking Dead comes to life," she added as Finley turned around to show off her zombie victim attire.

"Thanks. It was my kid's idea," Finley replied.

"Her daughter is one of the coolest teenagers I've ever met," Lillian added.

Finley smiled.

"Where are my manners?" Lillian chided herself. "Finley, this is Monica, a friend of mine from Miami. She works for the Port Authority."

"Nice to meet you," Finley said, holding out her hand.

"Let me guess, you're in the Coast Guard, too?" Monica replied, letting her hand linger a little too long.

"She's a rescue swimmer," Lillian added.

"Wow. No wonder you're in such great shape."

Finley smiled again. Monica was cute, and if she wanted to, Finley was pretty sure it wouldn't take much to bed the young woman. A one night stand was exactly what she usually wanted, no strings attached. She thought about it some more as she walked out of the kitchen, finally finding Tracey on the back patio.

"Sorry, didn't mean to leave you back there," Tracey said. "So…"

Finley raised an eyebrow. "So, what?"

"What did you think of Monica?"

"Oh, please don't tell me she came up here so you could set us up."

"What? No. I didn't even know she was a lesbian until she took one look at you and turned into a puddle on my kitchen floor," Tracey laughed.

"Seriously?"

"Yes!"

Finley grinned and shook her head.

Tracey saw Monica coming towards them. "Hey, I won't ask and you don't have to tell," she giggled, walking away.

Finley gave her a dirty look.

"You guys are pretty good friends, huh?" Monica asked.

"Yeah. You have to be on a different level when you do what we do. You're literally putting your life in other people's hands every time you go up in the helicopter."

"I'd put my life in your hands. In fact, I'd put all of me in your hands," Monica murmured.

Finley's eyebrows rose.

Monica chuckled. "Honestly, I'm not usually this forward. Maybe it's the one drink I've had."

Finley grinned. *If I take you home, it would be just another good time, followed by a lonely morning,* she thought. *Not tonight.* It wasn't like having a one-night stand was something new. She simply had other things on her mind lately. "I'm going to mingle for a bit and say hello to some people I haven't seen in a while. Maybe we can talk later," she said, trying to let the woman down easy.

Chapter 11

The long, skinny 737 airliner rolled to a stop outside of gate B3. Finley felt relieved to be on the ground, but her rolling stomach wouldn't settle down. She could fly in a helicopter for hours in bad weather with no problem, but there was something about being on a commercial plane that made her queasy. She unbuckled her seatbelt and waited. There were at least fifty people ahead of her, all trying to get off the plane at the same time. *I should've hitched a ride on a C-130,* she thought. Coast Guard personnel were always welcomed aboard as passengers on cargo planes. The only problem was finding a plane heading in the direction you needed to go and finding another one heading back. Since she was heading up to Charleston, the base that not only housed the AST Rescue Swimmer School, but was also the aviation hub for the Coast Guard, she usually had no problems hitching a ride. However, she had decided to fly commercial to make sure she arrived and departed in time to fit her tight schedule.

When the departure line finally began to move near the back of the plane, Finley snatched her bag out of the overhead compartment and followed the crowd into the terminal towards baggage claim. She'd fit everything she would need for the weekend, including her Service Dress Blue uniform for the parade, into her carry-on bag.

Checking her luggage was simply out of the question. She couldn't risk losing her SDB uniform.

As the crowd began to head towards the conveyer belt, Finley veered off towards the airport exit. She smiled when she saw her mother standing a few feet away, scanning the swarm of people.

"Looking for someone?" Finley teased, stepping up next to her.

"Oh, good lord!" Jackie Morris squeaked with surprise. "You damn near scared me half to death, Finley!"

"Sorry," Finley laughed, pulling her mother into a hug. "Let's get out of here. I'm starving."

"That's all you have?" Jackie asked, looking down at the carry-on bag.

"You'd be surprised at how much stuff I can fit into this thing."

Jackie nodded and led the way to her car. "Were you on shift today?" she asked.

"I'm on nights right now, so I got off this morning."

"Did you get any sleep before you left?"

"No," Finley replied.

Jackie nodded as she got into her car.

*

It didn't matter how many times she came home, or how long she stayed away. Every time Finley stepped foot in her old bedroom, the memories came flooding back. As she lay there, trying to nap, she reflected on the night Michael had died, and the first time she'd kissed Nicole. They'd been sitting on that same bed. The four walls of that room had seen so much, if only they could talk. She wondered what advice they'd give her. This was the worst part of coming home. Everything reminded her of Nicole and what seemed like a lifetime ago. *If I can't let you go, how in the hell am I ever going to move back here?* she thought.

Unable to sleep, Finley pulled on her sneakers, stuck her wallet in her pocket, and padded down the stairs. She was still dressed in the jeans and a dark blue t-shirt with SAR written in white on the upper left chest, that she'd worn on her flight.

"Do you mind if I borrow your car?" she asked.

Jackie looked up from the lesson plans she was working on for her class, at the dining table. She'd taken the day off since Finley was coming home, and with Veterans Day the next day, the school was closed anyhow. She was happy to have her daughter home, even if it was only from Thursday to Sunday. "Can't sleep?" she questioned.

"Nope."

Jackie smiled. "My keys are with my purse, on the coffee table."

"Do you need me to pick up anything?"

"No. I'll get dinner going while you're gone," Jackie replied.

Finley grabbed the keys and hugged her mother.

*

The short drive to Coast Guard Air Station Charleston, took about twenty minutes in the late afternoon traffic. Finley parked across the road from the main gate and turned the car off. Her eyes fixed on a red and white Coast Guard helicopter, hovering in the distance, more than likely doing some kind of aviation training. She wished she'd worn her uniform so that she could take a look around the Aviation Survival Training school, but she didn't have to step foot inside. She remembered the sights, smells, and sounds of that building like it was yesterday that she was there doing her own training. Those were some of the longest weeks and months of her life. If it hadn't been for the instructors challenging her to be better than the person beside her and forcing her to see the light at the end of the tunnel, she probably wouldn't be where she was today with her career. She wondered if she could do that...be that person for someone else. The person who takes someone to their limit, and dares them to go further.

Finley smiled, thinking about how much she'd hated those instructors. Today, she had the utmost respect for each and every one of them, especially the ones who pushed her when she nearly washed out in week four.

A tear rolled down her cheek when she thought about that day. She'd felt so alone. Knowing Nicole was in the same city, pregnant and scared, had torn Finley apart. She couldn't concentrate on anything. All she wanted to do was go home. When she failed a written test, then a water test two days later, she was taken aside by a female instructor who was a Petty Officer First Class.

"Morris, I don't know what's gotten into you, but you'd better get it out, and fast! Look around you. Do you not realize you're the best damn swimmer in this class? Hell, you're one of the best that has ever come through here! Listen to me kid, you are going to go places and do things that most women in the Coast Guard only dream about. You have so much potential. Don't throw it all away for nothing. You have to let go of whatever is bothering you. You'll never survive the next twenty weeks if you don't," she said.

"I will never let go. My partner is pregnant. She needs me. I shouldn't have come here," Finley replied.

"You came here for a reason. You wanted to be a rescue swimmer and save lives. You wanted to be somebody. Now is your time to do just that. Make your partner and child proud. You will leave your blood, sweat, and tears in this building, but what you take with you when you graduate is a lifetime of respect and admiration from your peers, and a sense of self-pride that no one, and nothing can take away from you. Remember that. Right here and right now is all about you, Finley. You can continue to forget why you chose to become a rescue swimmer and wash out, or you can get your ass back in that pool and show me why you are here."

*

"You were gone a while," Jackie said when Finley meandered inside.

"Sorry. I lost track of time."

"Are you nervous?" Jackie asked.

"Nervous? About what?"

"Caitlin marching tomorrow. I figured that's where you went. To go talk to her."

"I don't even know where they live," Finley replied, kicking off her shoes and sitting down at the dining table.

"They've been in Hickory Hills since Nicole married that sorry excuse for a man," Jackie said, placing their dinner on the table.

Finley nodded. "It figures they'd live on a golf course."

"Nicole doesn't play golf. They live there because of him. He thinks he's Tiger Woods or something."

Finley laughed.

"So, if you weren't with Caitlin, then where did you go for two hours?" Jackie questioned, between bites of food.

"The base."

"You weren't in your uniform. Did you have work to do?"

Finley set her fork down and folded her hands over her plate like a teepee. "I've been given the opportunity to become an instructor at the rescue swimmer school as my next transfer. It's a three year post like everything else."

"Really? That means you'd be moving back then, right?"

"Uh huh." Finley's eyes met her mother's. "I don't know if I can do it, Mom," she sighed. "Living away from here has helped me keep my sanity."

"I understand. Just because you live in the same city doesn't mean you and Nicole will be neighbors or bump into each other at the grocery store. Hell, I haven't seen her at all in the last seven years, except when it has to do with Caitlin." She set her fork down as well. "Is this even something you want to do? Be an instructor?"

"Yes. I wasn't expecting it right now. I actually wanted to finish out my career as an instructor, but this is a huge opportunity. I'd do it for three years, then go back into the field."

Jackie nodded. "You already know this, but Caitlin would be over the moon if you moved here. You'd be around for the rest of her high school years. It would actually benefit her in a lot of ways to have you close by. That kid practically worships the ground you walk on."

"I know." Finley smiled. "I've missed so much. The idea of being closer to Caitlin is great, but I can't be around Nicole."

"Who said you had to?"

"No one, but I have a pretty good idea how life is at her house. I don't think I could handle being in the same town the next time Caitlin tells me her mother is crying because that piece of trash screamed in her face. I'm liable to go over there and knock his ass out."

"Well, maybe that's a good thing." Jackie shrugged.

Finley grinned. "Seriously though, I haven't made any decisions. I have until the middle of next month."

"If you don't do the instructor thing, where will you be transferred to?"

"I have no idea. I put in for Savannah, to at least be a little closer. That was before the instructor thing came about. But, I'm a senior swimmer and a chief, so I'll get sent wherever I am needed most," she replied, going back to her dinner.

"At least you can't get shipped across the country or worse, the world. Patty, the vice principal at the school, her son is in the Army. He's stationed in Japan. She gets to see her grandkids once a year at most."

Finley scrunched her nose. The idea of being stationed in the middle of nowhere didn't appeal to her at all. "What does he do?" she asked.

"I don't know. He's some kind of supply officer or something. His wife went with him when he got transferred. They've been there for about three years, I think. She's an English teacher at a school in Okinawa."

Finley nodded.

"Either way, it's your life and your choice. I'm just glad you're here right now. We'll deal with the next three years when the time comes." Jackie smiled.

"Thanks, Mom."

Chapter 12

The next morning, Finley put on the navy-blue pants and light-blue, button-down shirt of her Service Dress Blue uniform. She checked the shine on her high-gloss oxford shoes before pulling them on. After that, she put on the dark-blue tab tie and pinned her rank insignia to both of her collar lapels. She checked her navy-blue coat one last time, making sure the four rows of ribbons and the aviation rescue swimmer badge above them, were perfectly placed on the left chest. Her last name and US Coast Guard were etched on the name tag on the opposite side. The coat also had a gold patch of her rank insignia on the upper left arm, and a patch with three gold stripes on the outside of the lower left arm, indicting at least twelve years of service.

Finley looked in the mirror as she pulled on the coat, fastening the three gold buttons down the center. There was something about getting dressed up in her fanciest uniform that made her back a little stiffer and forced her to stand a bit taller, giving her an overwhelming sense of pride.

She put her cover on her head, making sure it fit correctly since she rarely wore it. Most of her time was spent in a flight suit with a ball cap or garrison cap, not a formal cover. After one last check of her uniform in the mirror, she smiled and did an about-face.

"Wow," Jackie exclaimed, as her daughter stepped off the bottom of the staircase. "It's been a long time since I've seen you in your dress uniform. You've added more stuff to it, I see. I'm so damn proud of you," she added, wiping a tear from her cheek.

Finley smiled. "Thank you."

"We better get going before my make-up starts to run. You know how I hate to wear this stuff."

"Then, why do it?" Finley asked, locking the door behind them.

"Because, it's a special occasion," Jackie replied. "Why did you put on your dress uniform?"

"I don't think jeans and t-shirt are the proper attire to honor the veterans of this country, myself included."

"Exactly," Jackie stated, starting the car.

Finley furrowed her brow, unsure how make-up and a service dress uniform were on the same level.

"Are you going to be okay with Dave nearby?" Jackie asked, changing the subject.

"The parade goes for several blocks downtown. I seriously doubt we'll end up on the same street corner. Besides, Nicole has no idea I'm in town. I asked Caitlin not to say anything."

Jackie huffed. "She'd be stupid to think you would miss this."

Finley didn't comment as she watched the streets go by.

"Maybe he has a golf game he can't miss. I personally don't care to see him. Once in my lifetime was enough."

"When did you see him?" Finley questioned.

"Before they were married. He came outside when I was dropping Caitlin back at home."

"What does he look like?"

"Well, for starters, he's probably fifteen years older than Nicole, maybe more. I think he looks like George W. Bush, back when his hair was gray with a little bit of brown mixed in. He has similar beady eyes and a thin, cocky grin. He's about the same build, too. Maybe a couple inches shorter though."

"Sounds lovely," Finley muttered.

Jackie laughed as she pulled into an open parking space at a bank that was closed for the holiday. "This corner doesn't look as packed," she said, checking out the crowd. "I think it ends after the next block."

"It's fine with me," Finley replied, getting out of the car.

Jackie fell instep next to her daughter as they made their way towards the people who were lining both sides of the street. They walked a little further down, giving themselves a front row view from the corner curb.

"This is great. We'll be able to see everything," Jackie exclaimed, getting her phone ready to take pictures.

Finley shook hands with a few bystanders who took the time to thank her for her service, which she considered a nice gesture. By the time the marching bands were heard coming down the street, twice as many people had gathered around them.

Two high school bands and ROTC units passed by, followed by the Coast Guard band from the Charleston base. Behind them, was an Air National Guard regiment, and members from a few different VFW posts. People in the crowd cheered and yielded tiny American flags as the veterans waved.

"Here they come," Jackie said, noticing the Annandale High School banner in front of the band.

Finley watched the band go by, then turned her eyes to the Air Force ROTC unit marching behind them, being led by the color guard team. She quickly threw up a salute to the American flag, smiling proudly as her daughter passed by. *That's my girl*, she thought as she lowered her arm.

"There she is!" Jackie squealed, taking multiple pictures on her phone. As the group turned the corner, she moved to get a few more photos. "Nicole's here," she said, noticing the blond standing twenty feet away with her eyes glued to Finley.

"What? Where?" Finley questioned, looking around.

Finley froze in place as she locked eyes with the woman staring directly at her. It had been several years since she'd last seen Nicole in person. Her heart thumped loudly in her chest and a smile tugged on the corners of Finley's mouth. Nicole began to smile as well, but everything quickly faded as a gray-haired man grabbed her hand, shuffling her through the crowd.

"I guess she's gone," Jackie said, realizing Nicole had disappeared.

Finley stayed silent as they made their way towards the area zoned off for the end of the parade. A slew of parents headed in the same direction, looking for their children.

"Mom!" Caitlin yelled, waving at Finley through the crowd. "This is Major Bowman, my instructor. Major, this is my mother, Chief Petty Officer Finley Morris."

Finley shook his hand. "It's nice to meet you," she said.

"You're a Coast Guard rescue swimmer, am I right?"

"Yes," Finley smiled.

"It's an honor to finally meet you. I've heard a lot about you." He smiled. "That kid of yours is something special. As a freshman, she's moving through the ranks faster than anyone I've ever seen, and I've been instructing at Annandale for about six years now. I'm pretty sure she has her sights set on your job one day."

Finley grinned.

"Mom said it's okay for me to go to dinner with you and Grammy," Caitlin butted in.

Finley turned to see Nicole talking to her mother.

"Great. We'll take you home afterwards. I know you're going to your friend's birthday thing," Finley stated.

"How long are you in town for?" Caitlin asked.

"I leave on Sunday."

"Cool."

"We're all set," Jackie said, walking over to them. "Let me take a quick picture."

Finley stood at attention next to Caitlin. Then, wrapped her arm around her shoulders for the second picture.

"You look good, by the way," Jackie murmured as they began walking away.

Finley raised an eyebrow, giving her an odd look.

Jackie nodded towards the opposite direction, and Finley turned to see Nicole looking back at her, going the other way, with Dave pulling her along.

"It was nice meeting you, Chief. If you ever get some free time, I'd love to have you come talk to our cadets. It's good for them to learn about the different branches of service. In particular, the jobs within each branch," MAJ. Bowman said.

"I'm stationed down in Florida, but I can try to work something out for the next time that I visit," she said.

"Great. Here's my card. Just let me know."

Finley smiled and nodded as she slipped the card into her jacket pocket.

*

After dinner, Jackie drove Finley and Caitlin back to her house to eat some of the chocolate cake she'd made the day before.

"I still can't get over your dress uniform, Mom. It's so different than seeing you in a flight suit," Caitlin said, looking at Finley's service coat that was hanging on the back of one of the dining chairs. She'd changed her clothes as soon as they'd arrived at the house.

"The flight suit is a lot more comfortable."

Caitlin laughed. "What are all of those ribbons for? Do you have medals that go with them?"

Finley grabbed the coat and walked into the living room. Caitlin followed her like a little kid.

"Most of them have medals, yes. These were awarded to me and some of my units for different things like: Unit Commendation, Meritorious Unit Commendation, Meritorious Service, Humanitarian Service, Special Operations Service, Presidential Unit Citation, Leadership Achievement, Good Conduct, Basic Training Honor Graduate, Enlisted Person of the Year, Gold Lifesaving, Silver Lifesaving, and Distinguished Service. Most of them have been awarded multiple times over the years, which is why they have a tiny number, letter or symbol pinned on them," Finley explained, going over each one.

"Wow," Caitlin murmured.

"None of my medals or ribbons involve combat, which is something I'm thankful for. However, I risk my life day in and day out to save others, and I've been in a lot of hairy situations over the years. I've definitely earned each and every one of these. I wear them proudly," Finley said, draping her coat back over the chair. "You've seen what I do. It's not glamorous, and most of the time, it's very dangerous. These awards are nice to look at, but they're also a reminder of what I went through to earn them. Which is why it's nice to put on a real uniform once in a while. It helps me remember what I've accomplished in my years of service."

"How many more years do you think you'll stay in?" Caitlin asked.

"Oh, I don't know. I have about six and half more to go until I'm eligible for retirement, so at least that many." Finley smiled.

"I want to go all the way to retirement too," Caitlin replied.

"How about you get through four years of ROTC and then college, first."

"I know," Caitlin mumbled.

"I'm not ready for you to grow up so fast." Finley pulled her into a hug. "By the way, it was an honor to watch you march in that parade today. I'm glad I was able to come up for it," she said, letting go of her.

"Thanks. I'm glad you were here too. Maybe next time, you can come up for a swim meet."

141

"I'll see what I can do." Finley winked with a smile. "Come on, kiddo. I should probably get you home," she added, checking her watch.

"Do you want me to drive her?" Jackie asked.

"No. I'll do it," Finley replied, grabbing her mother's car keys.

Chapter 13

"Can we do something tomorrow," Caitlin asked as she called out the directions to where she lived.

"I don't see why not. What did you have in mind?"

Caitlin shrugged. "Here's the house," she said, pointing to the tan and brown, two-story house with a freshly manicured lawn. It was similar in stature to all of the other fancy houses along the golf course.

"This is nice," Finley said.

"It's Dave's," Caitlin muttered, rolling her eyes.

"Let me guess, he reminds you of that often."

"Oh, me and Mom, every chance he gets," Caitlin sighed.

Finley shook her head. "I'll call you in the morning, and we can figure out something to do."

"Sounds good. I love you, Mom."

"Love you, too, kiddo." Finley smiled, pulling her into a hug.

Nicole stepped out of the house and headed down the driveway as Caitlin got out of the car. Finley swallowed the lump in her throat. Nicole was just as beautiful as she had been the last time Finley laid eyes on her. Her honey-colored, blond hair hung loosely over one shoulder. The jeans and thin blouse she wore, hugged the subtle curves of her thin frame as she walked towards the car.

Nicole gasped in surprise when she realized Finley was in the driver's seat.

"Hello, Nic," Finley said softly. "I'm guessing you were expecting my mother," she added, noticing the change in her demeanor.

Nicole nodded. "It's been a long time," she murmured, avoiding Finley's questioning eyes. "She reminds me so much of you," she sighed, watching Caitlin enter the house.

"Don't hold that against her, because she's an amazing kid."

"I would never do that." Nicole looked into the same blue eyes that she saw every day in her daughter. "Can we go somewhere and talk?"

Shrugging, Finley nodded for her to get into the passenger seat.

"I'll be right back," Nicole uttered. She returned a few minutes later, sliding into the seat. "I had to make sure Dave was asleep for the night, and I told Caitlin I was stepping out. Her friend's mother should be here soon to pick her up anyway."

Finley didn't say anything as she put the car in reverse. She had no idea where to go, or what to say for that matter. She decided to go to the one place that always lifted her up when she felt down—Waterfront Park, a half-mile long section of the Cooper River with a fountain, benches, a floating dock, and a beautiful view of the waterway.

Finley pulled into a parking space and both women got out. The river water lapping against the dock looked black under the stars, with the nearly full moon glimmering in the distance.

"Caitlin is so much like you," Nicole muttered as they walked slowly along the path. "She doesn't just look like you. She has the same drive and determination with an all or nothing attitude. It scares me how similar you two are."

"She's a good kid, Nic. She should be allowed to make her own decisions. If she wants to follow in my footsteps, then so be it. It's her life and her choice," Finley stated. "But, just so you know, I'm pushing for her to go to college, not join the Coast Guard."

"That's good to know."

"She asked if she could live with me," Finley said, glancing at Nicole as they moved along the sidewalk, side by side at a snail's pace.

"What? When was this?" Nicole asked, slightly stunned.

"When she was with me over the summer," Finley replied as they stopped walking. "She's noticed a lot of problems in your house. Is she right?"

Nicole turned away. "I can't believe you're here," she whispered. "I've always wondered what it would be like when I saw you again." She wiped away a tear. "Today, when I saw you on that curb, standing proudly in your uniform, and then I watched our daughter march by, looking just as dignified in a uniform of her own, I realized the day was coming when she'd want to live with you." Nicole shook her head. "I can't lose her too," she cried, wiping away tears as they rolled down her cheek.

"You chose to lose me, and you chose this life," Finley said, stepping closer to her. "Tell me the truth, Nic. Is he mean to you?" she asked, rubbing a tear from Nicole's face with her thumb.

"Yes," Nicole whispered, almost too softly for Finley to hear.

Finley felt anger begin to boil in her stomach as her chest tightened. "Has he ever hit you?" she questioned.

"No," Nicole replied, shaking her head. "He's just verbally aggressive and yells a lot. He thinks you shouldn't be a part of Caitlin's life. That's mostly what we fight about."

"You don't deserve to be treated like that, and he damn sure doesn't deserve you," Finley murmured.

Nicole reached up, placing her hand on Finley's cheek. She rested it there for a second, before running it down her neck to the top of her chest. Finley wrapped her arms around Nicole, pulling her into a tight embrace. Nicole sighed deeply and sunk into the warm body against her.

Finley breathed in the long forgotten scent of Nicole's shampoo, mixed with a light, floral perfume. Her body trembled as she closed her eyes, reveling in the feel of Nicole in her arms.

The sound of a horn in the distance brought Finley back to reality. She quickly pulled away. "We should go," she said.

"I'll make arrangements for Caitlin to transfer schools, if that's what she wants to do. You can take her with you when you leave," Nicole stated.

Finley turned away, leaning on the rail and looking out over the dark water.

"What's wrong? I thought you'd be happy." Nicole moved to the rail beside her.

"I've been offered an instructor position at the rescue swimmer school as my next transfer post. I'm not sure I want to take it, but I need to have my decision made when I get back. Either way, in a month my next transfer will come up."

"Is that the swimmer school you went to? The one that's here?" Nicole asked.

"Yes."

"Well, that's great. You'll be nearby."

"I don't know if I'm going to take it." Finley looked over at her. "I'm not sure I can live that close to you."

"I don't understand. Why wouldn't you take a post that will bring you home?"

"It's not that easy for me. Why do you think you haven't seen me in so many years, Nic? It wasn't just you staying away. The cut is just as deep today as it was the day you walked out of my life," Finley said, sternly.

Nicole pushed off the rail. "We need to go. I should probably get home anyway."

"You always were one to run from a fight," Finley huffed.

"Don't bring up the past," Nicole said.

"Are we ever going to talk about it?" Finley asked, crossing her arms.

"I can't." Nicole shook her head and turned to walk away.

Finley quickly stepped around her. "Why not?"

Nicole didn't answer. Instead, she moved around Finley once more. But, Finley moved in front of her again.

"Damn it, Finley!"

"Why not, Nic? Why can't you talk about it?" Finley demanded.

"Because I'm still in love with you!" Nicole shouted. "I always have been and always will be. I've never been able to let you go," she whispered as her eyes welled with tears once more.

Finley stood in front of her, slightly stunned. She quickly grabbed Nicole, pulling her close. Their lips met in a gentle, probing kiss that quickly turned passionate.

Nicole wrapped her arms around Finley's neck, running her fingers into the back of her hair as their bodies rubbed together. Desperate to feel her, Finley pulled Nicole's shirt free of her pants, and slid her hands up and down the soft, smooth skin of her back.

"We can't do this here," Nicole breathed. Seeing the burning hunger in Finley's eyes, she looked back towards the car in the parking lot.

Finley let go of her and grabbed her hand. They covered the distance to the car as if their lives depended on it. Thankful they hadn't parked under a streetlight, Nicole quickly climbed into the backseat, pulling Finley in on top of her.

Clothes were removed as they frantically covered each other in bruising kisses. Finley reached Nicole's wet center first, sliding her fingers through the delicate folds. Nicole slammed her head back against the door and spread her legs as far as she could in the tight space when Finley moved down, replacing her fingers with her mouth.

"Oh, God," Nicole moaned, tugging on Finley's short curls.

Stopping before Nicole could release, Finley traced her tongue back up, suckling her breasts before kissing her hard. Nicole reached between them with one hand, pushing her fingers through Finley's wetness and deep inside of her. Her other hand skimmed her short nails up and down Finley's back as beads of sweat began to rise on her skin.

Finley bit her lower lip, forcing her racing heart to slow as her climax clawed at the edge. She slipped her fingers easily inside of Nicole, matching her movements, thrust for thrust. They rocked together, sliding in and out of each other in the cramped quarters as the windows began to fog from their heavy panting.

Nicole bit Finley's lip and moaned loudly as her body lost control. Finley roared a guttural sound and trembled, collapsing on top of her. They slowly pulled their hands free and their breathing eventually calmed.

Finley looked down into the hazel eyes staring back at her. She covered Nicole's lips with a soft, gentle kiss as Nicole ran her hands through the short, dark curls on the top of Finley's head.

Finley grinned when she looked up and saw a hand print on the foggy window. She realized they were literally stuck together as she began to move off of Nicole. The hot air in the car felt cool on their sweat-soaked skin as they gradually sat up, disentangling their limbs.

Nicole grabbed Finley's hand, checking the time on her wristwatch. "I need to get back," she said, sliding to the side and reaching for her clothes.

Finley stayed silent as she pulled her jeans and t-shirt on over her bra and underwear. She honestly didn't know what to say as she opened the back door, letting the breeze from the river inside the car. Nicole climbed out the opposite side and adjusted her clothing, before getting into the front passenger seat. Finley let out a long, deep breath as she pulled the driver's side door open.

The ride back across town was quiet. There wasn't much traffic on the streets, so the drive hadn't taken very long. Finley looked over at Nicole when she heard an audible sigh as they pulled into her driveway. "Are you okay?" she asked.

"Yes," Nicole answered, looking through the windshield.

"Where does this leave us?"

"I don't know," Nicole murmured, squeezing her eyes shut. "Let me know what you decide to do with your transfer. I won't say anything to Caitlin."

Finley nodded and watched her get out of the car. As soon as Nicole opened the front door of the house, Finley drove away. *What the hell have you done?* she thought.

*

The next morning, Jackie padded down the stairs to make breakfast. She noticed an empty rocks glass in the sink and walked over to the cabinet where she kept liquor stored for guests, since she wasn't a drinker herself. The bourbon bottle had been moved and was missing some of its contents.

"I knew seeing her was going to do you in," she sighed, shaking her head.

Jackie had just finished washing the glass out and putting it away when Finley appeared. She looked freshly showered and was dressed in jeans and a t-shirt.

"Everything okay?" Finley asked, noticing the odd expression on her mother's face.

"Yeah. You look chipper," Jackie mumbled, surprised to see her so awake and not hung over. She hated that Finley chose to indulge in alcoholic beverages, but she was old enough to make responsible decisions.

"I've been up for a bit. I jogged down to the coffee shop on the corner before the sun came up."

"Wow."

Finley laughed. "Mom, I'm up before the sun, exercising every day. I'm used to it."

Jackie nodded.

"I do have some bad news though. My CO called. I need to go back early. One of the swimmers in our unit had a family emergency. As the senior swimmer, it's my job to make sure we always have a swimmer on shift and on standby, with a relief. I have to go fill in."

"Well, I can't fault you for doing your job. Are you sure you're okay?"

"Yes. I'm fine. Is this about the glass you found in the sink? I only had two and I wasn't driving. I meant to wash it and put it away, but I was tired."

"I can't say anything about you having a drink, you're almost thirty-two years old. I just want to make sure you're okay. I'm more worried about what took you so long to take Caitlin home. I'm assuming you ran into Nicole."

"I did."

"And? How did that go?"

"I don't know. Not much was said, honestly. I told her about the instructor position."

"Does that mean you're taking it?"

Finley shook her head. "Probably not. She was going to let Caitlin come live with me. I had to tell her why she couldn't. Who knows where I'll wind up next."

"Wait, Caitlin wants to live with you?"

"Yes. She asked when she was down over the summer." Finley sighed, "Mom, I want to take her. I'd love to be around her every day, but my schedule is hectic, and she needs more than I can provide right now. Hell, I'm moving in a month and have no idea where I'm even going."

"What did Nicole say about you coming up here?"

"She thinks it's great, but what she doesn't realize is, it's only great for Caitlin and I, not Nicole and I."

"It sounds like you've got a lot to think about," Jackie said, pulling her into a hug. "I love you, and I know you'll do what's best for you."

"Thanks, Mom. Will you call Caitlin for me? We were supposed to get together today."

"I will. I'm sure she'll understand. What time does your flight leave?"

Finley looked at the clock on the stove. "I should probably get going. It leaves in two and a half hours."

"What about breakfast?"

"I'll be fine." Finley smiled. "You don't have to take me. I can call a cab or get an uber."

Jackie pinned her with a stern look that caused Finley to laugh. She remembered it well from her childhood. "Okay," she chuckled. "You can drive me."

Chapter 14

The next few weeks went by in a blur. Finley still hadn't decided what she wanted to do. She hadn't heard from Nicole, which was no surprise. She had probably been just as confused about what had happened between them. Finley picked up the phone to call her on several occasions, but had decided against it. She kept wondering why something that felt so right, had to be so wrong. And it was definitely wrong on multiple levels.

"It's Thanksgiving. There's nothing more to be thankful for than serving your country," Tracey said, standing at attention in front of the table full of food in the main hangar.

Finley laughed. "Uh, I'm thankful you know how to work a hoist; thankful Greg can fly an HH-65 in his sleep; thankful—"

"Okay, we get it," Tracey chuckled.

"I love my country, and I love what I do each and every day." Finley smiled like a cartoon. "Come on, let's get something to eat before the flies find this smorgasbord." She was happy to be spending at least part of the day with friends. She missed her family and had spoken to both her mother and Caitlin, who was over visiting with her, earlier in the day.

*

Around midnight, a nasty rainstorm blew in over the air station, leaving large puddles in its wake. The aircrew usually flew night missions, helping to spot drug boats that had made it past the Miami units. However, with the nasty storm, they'd been grounded, except for emergency call outs.

"I think it quit raining," Greg said, looking outside. "I checked the radar a little bit ago. The storm is headed east, southeast, so it'll clear us soon and be out to sea."

Finley was about to comment when the emergency siren went off.

"We've got a mayday, seventy-five miles off shore. A sailboat is taking on water and going down fast," the Operations Duty Officer said when the flight crew rushed into the dispatch office. "The weather hasn't let up much, so you'll be dealing with a pretty strong cross wind, heavy rain, and five to six foot seas."

"Roger," Greg replied. "We need to get in and get out. I don't want to be out in this mess any longer than we have to," he said to his crew as they prepped for takeoff.

As soon as the helo was in the air, Finley felt a knot form in the pit of her stomach. She'd flown in bad weather multiple times and had done numerous rescues in similar conditions, but the adrenaline rush was always higher in the middle of the night.

"Sector Merritt Island...Search and Rescue 6516. Be advised, our visibility range is less than two miles. Over."

"6516...Sector. Copy."

"This is going to be like trying to find a needle in a haystack while wearing a blindfold," Greg said.

"Try threading that needle blindfolded," Tracey added.

"Hey, watch who you're calling a needle," Finley teased, as they all searched the darkened sea with night vision goggles.

They were unable to fly at max speed because of the heavy winds, so it had taken longer than expected to reach the distressed boat. The waves were steady coming in at six feet, tossing the small sailboat all around. The mast had either been struck by lightning, or broken in the heavier storm winds that had passed over, because it was down and floating with the sail sheets just below the surface.

"Sector...6516. Be advised, we are on scene. The vessel is taking on water and listing heavily to port. The mast is down. Survivor is not visible. Over."

"6516...Sector. Copy. What are the current conditions? Over," the Operations Duty Officer asked.

"Sector...6516. Seas are holding at six foot with a moderate rain and fifteen knot crosswind. Over."

Greg turned on the floodlights and flew as low as he could over the boat, looking for the captain. After circling a few more times he radioed again.

"Sector...6516. The survivor may still be on board. There is no visual in the water. Over."

"6516...Sector. Copy. Deploy swimmer at your call. Over."

"Finley, I don't know about this," Greg said.

"I just saw a light in the starboard window," Tracey yelled into her radio. "He's inside."

"He has to be hurt," Finley replied. "Greg, I can get down to him and get him out. Will you be able to retrieve me?"

Greg checked the gauges again. The crosswind had picked up slightly. "We'll have one, maybe two shots."

"Let's do it," she said, sliding on the gunner belt and sitting down on the floor of the helo.

"Copy. Be safe, Finley," he said. "Flight Mech, prepare to deploy swimmer."

"Roger," Tracey replied, pulling open the cabin door.

Finley looked out at the pouring rain and closed her eyes. She took a deep breath and opened them, before connecting the hoist clasp to her survival harness.

Tracey tapped her on the chest to see if she was ready. Finley gave a quick thumbs up. Then, she pressed the button to raise the hoist, checking the weight load. She tapped Finley three times on the shoulder. Finley checked her harness, making sure the straps were all tight, before giving another thumbs up.

"Swimmer is ready."

"Deploy swimmer," he said, lowering the helo to fifty feet. Any lower and he'd risk the wind or waves causing an issue for Finley.

She went into the water on the face of a wave, quickly releasing the clasp as she rode it over to the boat.

"Swimmer is in the water and away," Tracey radioed, watching Finley climb up onto the starboard side of the sailboat, which was almost all the way out of the water.

"Hello? Captain?" Finley yelled, making her way towards the hatch. She smashed her fist down, pounding on it.

"Swimmer...6516. We are picking up a major crosswind. I'm going to lift up and regroup. Over," Greg radioed.

"6516...Swimmer. Copy," Finley replied, fighting to get the hatch open as the helo flew off in the distance. Finally able to get it open, she peered inside the cabin with her flashlight. The captain of the boat was slumped in the corner. "Sir, can you hear me?" she shouted.

The man nodded and pointed to his leg. Finley noticed his leg was broken with the bone slighting sticking out of the skin where the mast had split and smashed into him.

"I'm going to get you out of here, but we have to do it fast. The boats not going to float much longer," Finley said as she moved further inside. She checked his pulse and evaluated him as best she could with her flashlight.

"6516...Swimmer. I've located the survivor. He has a fractured tibia with a slight protrusion. Alert: 6; Injury: 8. Over."

"Swimmer...6516. Copy. Do you want us to deploy the litter or the basket? Over."

"6516...Swimmer. Send the litter," she radioed, trying to get the man into somewhat of a standing position on one leg.

"Swimmer...6526. Deploying litter."

Tracey attached the litter to the hoist and began to lower it down. The heavy crosswind caught the stretcher, sending it flailing about under the helo.

"Pull it up!" Greg yelled. "The wind is too strong."

Tracey quickly reversed the hoist, pulling the litter up. The wind caused it to smash into the side of the helo before she could bring it inside.

"Damn it!" Greg snapped. "Try the basket," he said to Tracey. "Swimmer...6516. We are in a major crosswind up here. Unable to deploy the litter. Switching to the basket. Over."

Finley didn't bother answering as she struggled to get the man to the other side of the cabin. The boat slowly rolled over, sending both of them crashing to the ground, slightly under water. "Sir, are you okay?" she called, trying to locate him in the nearly submerged vessel.

He reached out, grabbing her hand and she pulled him back up. Finley held onto him, tugging him along in the water with one arm while she shined the flashlight with the other, trying to find her way out.

Meanwhile, Tracey tried lowering the basket, which swung completely out of control. She had to quickly retrieve it. "We can't get anything down to her," she said, just as the fuel gauge alarm went off in the cockpit.

"Sector...6516. We are at bingo fuel in a thirty knot crosswind. Still trying to retrieve our swimmer and survivor. Over."

"6516...Sector. Copy. Return to base for refuel," the dispatcher said.

"Sector...6516. Negative on the return for fuel. We cannot leave our swimmer behind."

"6526...Sector. We've already called in the backup helo. Your swimmer will be retrieved. Return to base. Over."

"Son of a bitch!" Greg yelled. "Swimmer...6516. We're five minutes past bingo and being called in." He paused. "Finley, we can't get the basket or litter down to you. The crosswind is too strong."

"6526...Swimmer. Go back. I'll be right here when you return," she radioed as she finally pulled the man out of the boat.

"I see her!" Tracey yelled.

"Swimmer...6516. We have a visual. Deploying sling," he radioed. "Tracey, try to get the sling down to her."

The fuel alarm began wailing like a siren as Tracey connected the sling. As soon as it was below the helo, it too, began swinging wildly through the air.

"I can't get it down to her," she said.

Finley watched the sling wavering frantically around. "Greg, just go. If you wait any longer, you'll have to ditch," Finley radioed.

"Finley, I'm not leaving you, damn it!"

Tracey pulled the sling back inside, nearly falling out of the open cabin door as the wind blew the helo sideways.

"Drop three flares in the water and light her up," Greg said.

"Roger." Tracey quickly struck three flares, and tossed them down to water. They burst open, creating a bright orange glow.

"Sector...6516. We are inbound, ten minutes past bingo fuel. Swimmer and survivor have been marked with flares. Over," he radioed as they flew away.

Tracey watched the orange shimmering in the window until she could no longer see it.

*

Finley held the man backwards against her chest and pulled the attachment to inflate her vest. A loud pop sounded and the vest inflated in a split second. Because the vest was designed as a last measure, it was buoyant enough to keep her head out of water, but she still had to hold onto

159

the man and tread water to keep his head up. The boat had finally sunk just after the helo departed.

"Sir, stay with me. What's your name?" she asked.

"Harvey," he muttered.

"Okay, Harvey. Help is on the way," she said.

She slowly watched the flares die down until they were embers, knowing they were only thirty minute flares. Storm clouds lit up with lightning overhead, but thankfully, didn't drop any more rain as the large waves rocked and rolled her and Harvey further away from their last known location. She reached up with one hand, clicking on the emergency strobe light attached to her survival vest.

*

"Damn it, Commander. You have to let us go back out for her!" Greg yelled. "It's been two hours!"

"A cutter ship has been deployed and a C-130 is in the air. That's all we can do at this time. The conditions are too unstable for a helo right now. We'll get her, Greg. I promise." CDR. Douglas paced the floor of the dispatch office, remaining in contact with both the ship and plane.

*

Finley's arms burned with pain, and her hands were going numb from hanging onto the man. Her legs began to cramp as she fought the first stages of exhaustion and dehydration. She had no idea how long they'd been in the water. The last time she looked at her watch, it had been four and a half hours, but she could no longer move her arms enough to check again. Harvey had stopped answering when she spoke to him. She felt his chest moving where she

160

had her arms around him, so she knew he was breathing. She hoped he'd simply fallen asleep.

Come on, someone find me. This isn't how I want to go out, she thought as saltwater from another wave sprayed her in the face. The water temperature had dropped, indicating they'd been pushed further out to sea. Even though she was wearing a wetsuit, the seventy degree temperature had cooled her body tremendously.

Finley fought to keep her eyes open as the first ray of sunlight rose above the dark ocean. "Harvey, wake up," she mumbled, shaking him.

The man moved a little, but never said anything. She knew his body was in shock from the broken leg and hypothermia had more than likely set in by this point. Her mind drifted back to Caitlin and Nicole and the last time she'd seen either of them. She'd been so proud of the young woman Caitlin was becoming, and making love with Nicole, despite the circumstances, was the absolute last thing she ever thought would happen. Finley wondered if things truly did happen for a reason. *Did I get to see Caitlin march in that parade in my honor, and be intimate with Nicole one last time because I'm meant to die out here?* She thought as her teeth began to chatter.

*

Greg and Tracey had been flying around, searching for Finley since six a.m., after the winds had finally died down enough for them to get airborne. The ship had made it to the last known position, but there was no sign of the rescue swimmer or survivor. The C-130 had made passes all night, but were unable to find her in the dark water. The heavy cloud cover and intermittent rain showers hadn't helped with the search. Plus, the strong winds and waves of the storm had swept Finley much further out to sea than they'd expected, making her nearly impossible to find.

"She's been in the water for at least seven hours," Tracey said, scanning the ocean below.

"I know," Greg replied. "We'll find her. We have to."

"Sector Merritt Island…Search and Rescue 2112. We have a visual on the rescue swimmer. She has the survivor. Over," the pilot of the C-130 radioed, giving the coordinates.

"2112…Sector. Copy. Search and Rescue 6516…Sector. Did you pick up on those coordinates? Over."

"Sector…6516. Roger. Already en route," Greg radioed, pushing the helo to the maximum speed. "Thank God," he whispered. "Get ready, we're going to get our swimmer back!" he said to the crew, who cheered.

*

Finley was floating, with her head and the survivors just out of the water. The loud, thumping sound of a helicopter's rotor blade, caused her to crack open her eyes. She'd dreamed for hours of that sound and couldn't be more thankful to finally hear it. "Harvey, wake it! Help is here," she said, barely able to move herself. Before she knew it, she was being grabbed from behind.

"Chief, it's Petty Officer Talbot. I'm going to get you out of here," the rescue swimmer said. "Deploy the basket," he radioed. "Survivor Alert: 1; Injury: 10. Swimmer Alert: 4; Injury: 7. Over."

"Get that basket in the water," Greg said.

"I can't believe she never let go of that man," Tracey added as she quickly sent the basket out on the hoist. The dark blue water below was calm, almost completely flat as the sun shined brightly overhead in the cloudless sky. She said a silent prayer, thanking God that they'd found her friend.

"Me either," he replied, shaking his head in disbelief.

The swimmer practically stuffed Finley and Harvey into the basket in a heap of limbs and lifted his arm for them to get raised out of the water. As soon as she was in the helo, Finley's eyes finally closed as her body gave out.

Chapter 15

News crews were gathered for a press conference outside of the hospital later that afternoon as Captain Shultz described the heroic efforts of Helicopter Rescue Swimmer, Chief Petty Officer Finley Morris, when she not only rescued a distressed and injured sailor, Harvey Dunleavy, from his sinking boat, but treaded water, holding onto him to keep him afloat for over eight hours, until they could be rescued themselves after a severe storm.

"How is the rescue swimmer now?" one of the journalists asked.

"She's doing well. She suffered severe exhaustion, dehydration, and hypothermia, but she will make a full recovery." He smiled.

"What about the man she rescued?" someone else asked.

"Mr. Dunleavy was overwhelmed with severe hypothermia and dehydration, and he suffered a broken leg when the storm snapped the mast on his sailboat. I've been told that he too, will make a full recovery, thanks to the dedication of Chief Morris."

*

"You're on the news," Tracey said, sitting down in the chair next to Finley's hospital bed.

"I know," Finley replied. "How is Mr. Dunleavy?"

"He got out of surgery a little while ago. I think they had to put a rod or pins in his leg, but he should recover fine."

Finley nodded. "When are they going to let me out of here?"

"The doctor told me possibly this evening, If not, it will be tomorrow."

"I'm fine," Finley mumbled. "Just tired."

"That's why they told you to get some sleep."

"I did! I slept for a few hours. It's almost dark outside," Finley huffed. "I still feel like I'm in that damn water," she whispered.

Tracey patted her hand then walked out into the hallway as Finley's room phone rang.

"Hello?" she answered.

"Mom?"

"Caitlin?"

"Oh, my God, Mom! Are you okay?" Caitlin cried.

"Yes, kiddo. I'm fine, just a little tired."

"You've been all over the news."

"So, I've heard."

"Did you really tread water while holding onto that man all night?"

"Yes."

"Mom, that's crazy."

"It's my job, Caitlin."

"I know...I just...I can't believe it. Are you sure you're okay?"

"I promise I'm fine."

"Mom has been hysterical. We're over at Grammy's house."

"Caitlin, do me a favor, go and give her a big hug from me and tell her that I'm okay."

"Alright. Do you want to talk to her?"

Fearing that would only upset both herself and Nicole, especially since she was still confused about everything that had happened, she said, "No. The doctor just came in. I'll call you when I go home."

"You're going home today?" Caitlin questioned with surprise in her voice.

"Yes. I told you, I'm fine. I love you. I'll call you later tonight or first thing in the morning." She hung up, staring at the empty room. The one voice she'd wanted to hear more than anything during her ordeal at sea, was the one voice she couldn't bear to hear since being found. She wasn't sure she could handle the rejection she was sure to face. Reality had obviously slapped Nicole across the face because she hadn't heard from her at all since their night together.

"Good news!" Tracey exclaimed, barreling into the room. "You're being released!"

"Thank God," Finley uttered. "I just want to go home."

"I don't blame you. Our flight crew is on leave for the next two days, per the captain."

"Really?"

"Leaving you out there wasn't easy…on any of us. Greg has taken it pretty hard."

"Tracey, I told him to leave me. If he hadn't listened, you guys would've had to ditch or risk crashing. He did the right thing."

"He knows that. I know that. It doesn't make it any easier."

"Hey, you guys found me…eventually," Finley teased, trying to lighten the mood. "I'll be fine. That is what I am trained to do. It's my job."

*

Two days later, Finley put the finishing touches on the service coat of her Full Dress Blue uniform. It was basically the same uniform she'd worn to the Veterans Day parade, except the shirt was white instead of light blue, and her coat was adorned with her medals instead of the ribbon board. She was being awarded the Coast Guard Medal, which was the highest medal you could earn for a voluntary act of heroism or bravery in the face of great personal danger, not involving actual conflict with an enemy. She checked the decorations on her coat one last time, and was about to pull it on when her doorbell rang.

Greg was standing on the other side wearing his FDB uniform, when she pulled the door open. She smiled and waved him inside.

"It's about time you came around," she said.

"I don't know what to say, other than I'm sorry," he replied earnestly.

Finley had never seen such a somber look in his eyes. "Greg, you did your job. I did my job. That's what we're trained to do. It was no one's fault, especially not yours. I told you to go."

"I know you did, but I outrank you. I should've stayed and tried something else. We should've been able to retrieve you."

Finley shook her head and sighed. "You know you couldn't get to me. If you'd have waited any longer, the

Coast Guard would be hosting four funerals right now, instead of giving me another medal."

"Yeah, congrats on that by the way. The Coast Guard Medal is a big deal."

"Thank you for finally coming to get me. Otherwise, my family would be getting it." She smiled, patting him on the shoulder.

"Any time. That's what I'm there for, retrieving your butt when you go swimming." He grinned.

Finley laughed, pulling him into a hug. "You did your job, and I wouldn't have wanted you to do it any other way. If I had died out there while waiting for you to return, it would've been an honor because I would've died doing what I love," she said seriously.

"I know," he whispered. "Come on, let's go get you another decoration," he said, pulling away and standing up straight.

"You need to catch up," she teased, looking at his uniform. "And you call yourself an officer." She shook her head playfully.

"Hey, we can't all be as great as you!" he retorted with a smile as he watched her put on her coat and button the gold buttons.

*

The award ceremony was full of pomp and circumstance. The entire air station was on hand in full dress. The local news crew was there, filming and conducting a few brief interviews with the high-ranking personnel of the district and air station, as well as Finley. She felt like it was all too much, but she was honored to be recognized for what she'd done. When the rear admiral of her Coast Guard district presented her with the medal, she saw nothing but respect from her peers, subordinates, and commanders as they stood at attention, saluting her.

After a few pictures of her and the medal with the rear admiral, CAPT. Shultz, CDR. Douglas, CMC. Newberry, and a few others, Finley made her way over to a man in a wheelchair that she'd noticed when she was up on the stage.

"Mr. Dunleavy," Finley said, stepping up next to him.

"Please, call me Harvey," he replied, reaching out to shake her hand. "They should give you a lot more than just a medal," he added, pointing to the velvet box in her hand.

Finley smiled. "This will do."

"Honestly, Chief Morris. Thank you for never letting go of me out of there. You risked your own life to save mine, and my family and I will be forever thankful for you," he stated, squeezing her hand.

"You're welcome," she said, bending down to hug him.

*

Once the celebration had concluded, Finley found herself in CMC. Newberry's office.

"What you did the other day was more than heroic, Finley. I'll never know how you were able to hold on to that man, while keeping both of your heads above water, for nearly nine hours." He shook his head.

"I don't know either," she sighed. "I just knew I was never letting go of him." She looked up at the wall behind the desk where the Coast Guard motto: *Semper Paratus*

Always Ready, was written below the Coast Guard logo. The words: *So Others May Live,* were etched below it.

CMC. Newberry followed her eyes and smiled. "I'm pretty sure I know why you're in here."

Finley nodded. "I'd fly out on a call and jump in the water right now, if I was needed," she said.

"I know that. Hell, we all know that. Whether that situation the other day happened or not, I think you're making the right decision, personally and for your career."

"Just so you know, I was leaning in this direction before the events of the other day. I love my job, and if I can help make those coming behind me as good, or even better than I am, then I feel like that's also my job."

"Between you and I, this doesn't leave this room," he said. "You're well on your way to making senior chief."

"Really?" she said, a little surprised.

"Absolutely. People talk and the only way to get into the higher ranks is recognition. When you get recommended for senior chief, and the paperwork comes across his desk to allow or deny the request, the rear admiral will remember your name. He'll remember this day. Not because you are a woman, but because of the distinguished service you provided to earn that medal."

Finley nodded in understanding.

"I know your post here isn't up for another six weeks, but there is a new class starting in two weeks at the training center. I spoke to both Commander Hill, the executive officer, and Command Master Chief Wright. They would like you to report before that time so that you can get acquainted with everyone and settle into your new position."

"Wow."

"They are eager to meet you and think you will be a great role model. In my opinion, you'll be a lead instructor in no time," he said with a grin.

"Thank you for everything that you've done for me," Finley said, shaking his hand.

"It's been an honor serving with you," he replied.

Finley stood up and walked out of his office. Captain Shultz was standing nearby.

"I assume we're losing you a few weeks early," he said.

"Yes, sir."

"Those incoming cadets have no idea how much of an impact you are going to have on their careers. The ones who succeed and become swimmers, will be better at their jobs because of you. The ones who wash out, will have the utmost respect for you," he stated.

"Thank you."

"You are welcome back to Air Station Merritt Island any time," he added, shaking her hand.

Chapter 16

Finley had never packed her belongs so quickly in her life. Thankfully, the house had come furnished, so all she had was her personal possessions, and a few odds and ends. She'd already given the landlord notice that she'd be out by the last week of December, so moving a couple of weeks early hadn't been a big deal.

After a quick goodbye to the neighbor she'd gotten to know so well during Caitlin's visit, she closed the door to her loaded down SUV and backed out of the driveway. She smiled at the *Oasis* as she drove past it and turned into another shopping center a few blocks down.

*

"Those doughnuts are going to kill you one day," Finley said, sliding into the booth next to Greg.

"He thinks they're better than drinking an energy drink or a triple shot of espresso," Tracey added, sitting across from them.

Finley laughed.

"I hate that you're leaving," Tracey said.

"Aren't you right behind me?" Finley questioned.

"Yeah. I have about two months left on post. I found out yesterday that I'm going to Clearwater."

"Oh, that's not bad. At least they didn't send you north."

"True."

"I still have two more years here," Greg stated.

"I forgot you chose to remain on post last year and they accepted it. That rarely happens," Finley said.

"Are you excited or nervous?" Tracey asked.

"I don't know. A little bit of both, I guess. Nervous about going home. I'm not sure how all of that will play out. I'm excited about seeing my daughter more, I know that. As far as the swimmer school...I'm going to miss being in the air and jumping out of helos, but I think I'm going to enjoy barking orders and modeling the next generation of rescue swimmers into shape." She smiled.

"It's only for three years. You'll be back in the air in no time. Just look at how fast this post went by," Tracey said. "And who knows, maybe we'll all meet up again at our next transfer."

Finley smiled and stood up, hugging both of her friends. She grabbed a doughnut out of the box for the road. "Be safe up there, both of you," she said.

"Roger," Greg replied.

"Text me when you get there, so I know you made it safely. I'd rather be in the air than on the roads," Tracey said.

Finley smiled and waved as she walked out the door. She'd made plans to keep in contact with both of them, and she knew she would. She was still in contact with people she'd flown with at all of her posts. Many of whom had called her after seeing her in the news. She slid into the driver's seat of her SUV, turned the radio, and settled in for the long drive home. It felt so odd to actually be going 'home'. She had no idea what to expect when she got there.

All she knew was her mother had said she could stay with her indefinitely if that's what she wanted. Although, she'd planned to quickly find a place closer to the base.

*

The six-hour drive had taken more like seven and a half with traffic, as well as stops for food and gas. Finley pulled into her mother's driveway and stretched her stiff muscles. Figuring she could unload the car later, she grabbed her cell phone and her keys, and meandered up the walkway.

"Mom, it's me," she said, knocking on the door.

Finley's jaw hit the floor when the lock clicked and the door swung open. Nicole was standing there, looking quite comfortable in an old pair of jeans and a t-shirt, with no shoes.

"What are you doing here?" Finley asked, stepping inside.

"Your mom took Caitlin to the movies so we could have some time to talk."

"What's there to talk about?" Finley said as she walked into the living room, setting her keys and phone on the table. She turned back to look at Nicole and as she stepped closer, she noticed tears in her eyes.

"I'm so proud of you for saving that man's life," Nicole murmured. "But, don't you ever jeopardize your own life like that again. We need you too much," she finished as a few tears rolled down her cheek.

"What do you mean by we?" Finley asked.

Nicole wrapped her arms around Finley, kissing her softly. Finley melted into her, allowing the contact, before backing away.

174

"I can't do this," Finley said. "I'm not going to have you on the side." She shook her head. "I've loved you since I was fifteen years old. It's all or nothing with me. You know that."

"That's good," Nicole murmured, grabbing her hands. "Because I'm never walking away from you again. I filed for divorce the week after you left, and Caitlin and I moved in here."

"What?" Finley questioned, slightly stunned.

"I made Caitlin promise not to say anything when she talked to you."

"Why didn't you say something?"

"I didn't know how or what to say. All I know is I never let go. I've never stopped loving you. I made a huge mistake by allowing my mother to control my life. Seeing you at that parade made me realize how much I missed you. Being with you that night made me also realize that you still loved me too. I knew it wasn't too late, that I hadn't lost you," Nicole said as a few more tears rolled down her cheek. "I met with my lawyer on Monday and called your mother on my way home. We had a long talk and she told me to bring Caitlin and move in with her."

"I…" Finley stumbled for words. She closed her eyes and opened them to make sure she wasn't dreaming. "I don't know what to say," she mumbled.

"Say you want to be a family again," Nicole said, smiling through her tears. "I love you, Finley. I belong with you, wherever you are. I always have and I always will."

Finley wrapped her arms around Nicole, picking her up off the ground. "I love you so damn much!" she whispered, before kissing her.

"So that's a yes?" Nicole grinned.

"Absolutely. I'm never letting you go again," Finley replied, kissing her once more.

About the Author

Graysen Morgen is the bestselling author of *Falling Snow*, *Fast Pitch*, *Cypress Lake*, the Bridal Series: *Bridesmaid of Honor*, *Brides*, and *Mommies*, as well as many other titles. She was born and raised in North Florida with winding rivers and waterways at her back door, and the white sandy beach a mile away. She has spent most of her lifetime in the sun and on the water. She enjoys reading, writing, fishing, coaching and watching soccer, and spending as much time as possible with her wife and their daughter.

Email: graysenmorgen@aol.com
Facebook.com/graysenmorgen
Twitter: @graysenmorgen
Instagram: @graysenmorgen

Other Titles Available From Triplicity Publishing

Pursuit by Joan L. Anderson. Claire is a workaholic attorney who flies to Paris to lick her wounds after being dumped by her girlfriend of seventeen years. On the plane she chats with the young woman sitting next to her, and when they land the woman is inexplicably detained in Customs. Claire is surprised when she later runs into the woman in the city. They agree to meet for breakfast the next morning, but when the woman doesn't show up Claire goes to her hotel and makes a horrifying discovery. She soon finds herself ensnared in a web of intrigue and international terrorism, becoming the target of a high stakes game of cat and mouse through the streets of Paris.

Wrecked by Sydney Canyon. To most people, the *Duchess* is a myth formed by old pirates tales, but to Reid Cavanaugh, a Caribbean island bum and one of the best divers and treasure hunters in the world, it's a real, seventeenth century pirate ship—the holy grail of underwater treasure hunting. Reid uses the same cunning tactics she always has before setting out to find the lost ship. However, she is forced to bring her business partner's daughter along as collateral this time because he doesn't trust her. Neither woman is thrilled, but being cooped up on a small dive boat for days, forces them to get know each other quickly.

Arson by Austen Thorne. Madison Drake is a detective for the Stetson Beach Police Department. The last thing she wants to do is show a new detective the ropes,

178

especially when a fire investigation becomes arson to cover up a murder. Madison butts heads with Tara, her trainee, deals with sarcasm from Nic, her ex-girlfriend who is a patrol officer, and finds calm in the chaos of police work with Jamie, her best friend who is the county medical examiner. Arson is the first of many in a series of novella episodes surrounding the fictional Stetson Beach Police Department and Detective Madison Drake.

Change of Heart by KA Moll. Courtney Holloman is a woman at the top of her game. She's successful, wealthy, and a highly sought after Washington lobbyist. She has money, her job, booze, and nothing else. In quiet moments, against her will, her mind drifts back to her days in high school and to all that she gave up. Jack Camdon is a complex woman, and yet not at all. She is also a woman who has never moved beyond the sudden and unexplained departure of her high school sweetheart, her lover, and her soul mate. When circumstances bring Courtney back to town two decades later, their paths will cross. Will it be too late?

Mommies (Bridal Series book 3) by Graysen Morgen. Britton and her wife Daphne have been married for a year and a half and are happy with their life, until Britton's mother hounds her to find out why her sister Bridget hasn't decided to have children yet. This prompts Daphne to bring up the big subject of having kids of their own with Britton. Britton hadn't really thought much about having kids, but her love for Daphne makes her see life and their future together in a whole new way when they decide to become mommies.

Haunting Love by K.A. Moll. Anna Crestwood was raised in the strict beliefs of a religious sect nestled in the foothills of the Smoky Mountains. She's a lesbian with a ton of baggage—fearful, guilty, and alone. Very few things would compel her to leave the familiar. The job offer of a lifetime is one of them. Gabe Garst is a police officer. She's also a powerful medium. Her work with juvenile delinquents and ghosts is all that keeps her going. Inside she's dead, certain that her capacity to love is buried six feet under. Anna and Gabe's paths cross. Their attraction is immediate, but they hold back until all hope seems lost.

Rapture & Rogue by Sydney Canyon. Taren Rauley is happy and in a good relationship, until the one person she thought she'd never see again comes back into her life. She struggles to keep the past from colliding with the present as old feelings she thought were dead and gone, begin to haunt her. In college, Gianna Revisi was a mastermind, ring-leading, crime boss. Now, she has a great life and spends her time running Rapture and Rogue, the two establishments she built from the ground up. The last person she ever expects to see walk into one of them, is the girl who walked out on her, breaking her heart five years ago.

Second Chance by Sydney Canyon. After an attack on her convoy, Marine Corps Staff Sergeant, Darien Hollister, must learn to live without her sight. When an experimental procedure allows her to see again, Darien is torn, knowing someone had to die in order for this to happen.
She embarks on a journey to personally thank the donor's family, but is too stunned to tell them the truth. Mixed

emotions stir inside of her as she slowly gets to the know the people that feel like so much more than strangers to her. When the truth finally comes out, Darien walks away, taking the second chance that she's been given to go back to the only life she's ever known, but she's not the only one with a second chance at life.

Meant to Be by Graysen Morgen. Brandt is about to walk down the aisle with her girlfriend, when an unexpected chain of events turns her world upside down, causing her to question the last three years of her life. A chance encounter sparks a mix of rage and excitement that she has never felt before. Summer is living life and following her dreams, all the while, harboring a huge secret that could ruin her career. She believes that some things are better kept in the dark, until she has her third run-in with a woman she had hoped to never see again, and gives into temptation. Brandt and Summer start believing everything happens for a reason as they learn the true meaning of meant to be.

Coming Home by Graysen Morgen. After tragedy derails TJ Abernathy's life, she packs up her three year old son and heads back to Pennsylvania to live with her grandmother on the family farm. TJ picks back up where she left off eight years earlier, tending to the fruit and nut tree orchard, while learning her grandmother's secret trade. Soon, TJ's high school sweetheart and the same girl who broke her heart, comes back into her life, threatening to steal it away once again. As the weeks turn into months and tragedy strikes again, TJ realizes coming home was the best thing she could've ever done.

Special Assignment by Austen Thorne. Secret Service Agent Parker Meeks has her hands full when she gets her new assignment, protecting a Congressman's teenage daughter, who has had threats made on her life and been whisked away to a Christian boarding school under an alias to finish out her senior year. Parker is fine with the assignment, until she finds out she has to go undercover as a Canon Priest. The last thing Parker expects to find is a beautiful, art history teacher, who is intrigued by her in more ways than one.

Miracle at Christmas by Sydney Canyon. A Modern Twist on the Classic Scrooge Story. Dylan is a power-hungry lawyer who pushed away everything good in her life to become the best defense attorney in the, often winning the worst cases and keeping anyone with enough money out of jail. She's visited on Christmas Eve by her deceased law partner, who threatens her with a life in hell like his own, if she doesn't change her path. During the course of the night, she is taken on a journey through her past, present, and future with three very different spirits.

Bella Vita by Sydney Canyon. Brady is the First Officer of the crew on the Bella Vita, a luxury charter yacht in the Caribbean. She enjoys the laidback island lifestyle, and is accustomed to high profile guests, but when a U.S. Senator charters the yacht as a gift to his beautiful twin daughters who have just graduated from college and a few of their friends, she literally has her hands full.

Brides (Bridal Series book 2) by Graysen Morgen. Britton Prescott is dating the love of her life, Daphne Attwood, after a few tumultuous events that happened to unravel at her sister's wedding reception, seven months earlier. She's happy with the way things are, but immense pressure from her family and friends to take the next step, nearly sends her back to the single life. The idea of a long engagement and simple wedding are thrown out the window, as both families take over, rushing Britton and Daphne to the altar in a matter of weeks.

Cypress Lake by Graysen Morgen. The small town of Cypress Lake is rocked when one murder after another happens. Dani Ricketts, the Chief Deputy for the Cypress Lake Sheriff's Office, realizes the murders are linked. She's surprised when the girl that broke her heart in high school has not only returned home, but she's also Dani's only suspect. Kristen Malone has come back to Cypress Lake to put the past behind her so that she can move on with her life. Seeing Dani Ricketts again throws her off-guard, nearly derailing her plans to finally rid herself and her family of Cypress Lake.

Crashing Waves by Graysen Morgen. After a tragic accident, Pro Surfer, Rory Eden, spends her days hiding in the surf and snowboard manufacturing company that she built from the ground up, while living her life as a shell of the person that she once was. Rory's world is turned upside when a young surfer pursues her, asking for the one thing she can't do. Adler Troy and Dr. Cason Macauley from Graysen Morgen's bestselling novel: *Falling Snow*, make an appearance in this romantic adventure about life, love, and letting go.

Bridesmaid of Honor (Bridal Series book 1) by Graysen Morgen. Britton Prescott's best friend is getting married and she's the maid of honor. As if that isn't enough to deal with, Britton's sister announces she's getting married in the same month and her maid of honor is her best friend Daphne, the same woman who has tormented Britton for years. Britton has to suck it up and play nice, instead of scratching her eyes out, because she and Daphne are in both weddings. Everyone is counting on them to behave like adults.

Falling Snow by Graysen Morgen. Dr. Cason Macauley, a high-speed trauma surgeon from Denver meets Adler Troy, a professional snowboarder and sparks fly. The last thing Cason wants is a relationship and Adler doesn't realize what's right in front of her until it's gone, but will it be too late?

Fate vs. Destiny by Graysen Morgen. Logan Greer devotes her life to investigating plane crashes for the National Transportation Safety Board. Brooke McCabe is an investigator with the Federal Aviation Association who literally flies by the seat of her pants. When Logan gets tangled in head games with both women will she choose fate or destiny?

Just Me by Graysen Morgen. Wild child Ian Wiley has to grow up and take the reins of the hundred year old family business when tragedy strikes. Cassidy Harland is a little surprised that she came within an inch of picking up a gorgeous stranger in a bar and is shocked to find out that stranger is the new head of her company.

Love Loss Revenge by Graysen Morgen. Rian Casey is an FBI Agent working the biggest case of her career and madly in love with her girlfriend. Her world is turned upside when tragedy strikes. Heartbroken, she tries to rebuild her life. When she discovers the truth behind what really happened that awful night she decides justice isn't good enough, and vows revenge on everyone involved.

Natural Instinct by Graysen Morgen. Chandler Scott is a Marine Biologist who keeps her private life private. Corey Joslen is intrigued by Chandler from the moment she meets her. Chandler is forced to finally open her life up to Corey. It backfires in Corey's face and sends her running. Will either woman learn to trust her natural instinct?

Secluded Heart by Graysen Morgen. Chase Leery is an overworked cardiac surgeon with a group of best friends that have an opinion and a reason for everything. When she meets a new artist named Remy Sheridan at her best friend's art gallery she is captivated by the reclusive woman. When Chase finds out why Remy is so sheltered will she put her career on the line to help her or is it too difficult to love someone with a secluded heart?

In Love, at War by Graysen Morgen. Charley Hayes is in the Army Air Force and stationed at Ford Island in Pearl Harbor. She is the commanding officer of her own female-only service squadron and doing the one thing she loves most, repairing airplanes. Life is good for Charley, until the day she finds herself falling in love while fighting for her life as her country is thrown haphazardly into World War II. Can she survive being in love and at war?

Fast Pitch by Graysen Morgen. Graham Cahill is a senior in college and the catcher and captain of the softball team. Despite being an all-star pitcher, Bailey Michaels is young and arrogant. Graham and Bailey are forced to get to know each other off the field in order to learn to work together on the field. Will the extra time pay off or will it drive a nail through the team?

Submerged by Graysen Morgen. Assistant District Attorney Layne Carmichael had no idea that the sexy woman she took home from a local bar for a one night stand would turn out to be someone she would be prosecuting months later. Scooter is a Naval Officer on a submarine who changes women like she changes uniforms. When she is accused of a heinous crime she is shocked to see her latest conquest sitting across from her as the prosecuting attorney.

Vow of Solitude by Austen Thorne. Detective Jordan Denali is in a fight for her life against the ghosts from her past and a Serial Killer taunting her with his every move. She lives a life of solitude and plans to keep it that way. When Callie Marceau, a curious Medical Examiner, decides she wants in on the biggest case of her career, as well as, Jordan's life, Jordan is powerless to stop her.

Igniting Temptation by Sydney Canyon. Mackenzie Trotter is the Head of Pediatrics at the local hospital. Her life takes a rather unexpected turn when she meets a flirtatious, beautiful fire fighter. Both women soon discover it doesn't take much to ignite temptation.

One Night by Sydney Canyon. While on a business trip, Caylen Jarrett spends an amazing night with a beautiful stripper. Months later, she is shocked and confused when that same woman re-enters her life. The fact that this stranger could destroy her career doesn't bother her. C.J. is more terrified of the feelings this woman stirs in her. Could she have fallen in love in one night and not even known it?

Fine by Sydney Canyon. Collin Anderson hides behind a façade, pretending everything is fine. Her workaholic wife and best friend are both oblivious as she goes on an emotional journey, battling a potentially hereditary disease that her mother has been diagnosed with. The only person who knows what is really going on, is Collin's doctor. The same doctor, who is an acquaintance that she's always been attracted to, and who has a partner of her own.

Shadow's Eyes by Sydney Canyon. Tyler McCain is the owner of a large ranch that breeds and sells different types of horses. She isn't exactly thrilled when a Hollywood movie producer shows up wanting to film his latest movie on her property. Reegan Delsol is an up and coming actress who has everything going for her when she lands the lead role in a new film, but there one small problem that could blow the entire picture.

Light Reading: A Collection of Novellas by Sydney Canyon. Four of Sydney Canyon's novellas together in one book, including the bestsellers Shadow's Eyes and One Night.

Visit us at www.tri-pub.com

60788204R00118

Made in the USA
Lexington, KY
18 February 2017